DEAD MAN'S LIST

A DANNY CORTEZ THRILLER
BOOK 1

L.T. RYAN

WITH
ANDRE GONZALEZ

For Natasha.
Thank you for always making things happen.

THE DANNY CORTEZ SERIES

Dead Man's List
Shadow Directive
Widow Protocol

CHAPTER
ONE

DANNY CORTEZ EXAMINED the paper on his mother's nightstand, as if the ink were burning a hole in the wood beneath it. They wanted him dead.

The handwritten note, no bigger than a credit card, lay open beneath a vase of colorful flowers. "Ma, who did you say sent these flowers?" Danny rubbed his forehead, anxiety creeping into his veins as he kept staring at the name written on the note.

"I'm not sure," his mother replied from the recliner in the corner of her room. Danny had spent the past few years bouncing around the country, staying under the radar as much as possible. But given his mother's condition, he needed to stay connected with a cell phone at the least. His last mission as an agent for the DEA had left Danny's life in shambles. Sure, he'd expected some hardships after putting powerful criminals behind bars, but he never thought he'd spend his life hiding from a drug cartel.

Assigning the alias of Ana Garcia to his mother didn't make matters any easier for her deteriorating mental health, but he couldn't take a chance. She was all he had left. Her real name was Tatiana Cortez, but no one inside the confines of the Morning Star Retirement Community knew that. They had found Tatiana a home here. With medical care to ease her transition into dementia, Danny didn't have to worry as much while away.

No matter where Danny was hiding, he always came to visit his mother on the first day of every month. His mind raced, the note glaring back at him. He had to move his mother if their actions were exposed. Change his visiting routine. Even change aliases. The thought of dealing with all of that right now made him want to puke.

"Ma, I need to know," Danny pressed on. "Who brought these flowers into your room?"

"One of the nurses, Daniel." She stared blankly at the muted TV hanging on the wall, showing an episode of *Wheel of Fortune*. "Why are you being so pushy?"

"We've talked about this. Remember?"

She nodded slowly, but Danny had no idea how much of anything she remembered these days. The first signs had come two years ago, when she'd called Danny frequently about misplacing things around the house, asking him to come help her. He'd swing by and find her car keys in the silverware drawer. Wallet in the dirty clothes hamper. A bowl of cereal in the microwave. Seeing those things drew immediate concern and worry, as they would for any caring son. But when Tatiana Cortez couldn't even remember the name of her late husband, Danny had gone through a mental breakdown of his own before seeking professional help for her.

She waved him off. "Yes, I remember. Why are you so interested in my flowers? There are some kind people out there who randomly send us flowers. Or candies. Books. Socks. You name it."

This didn't surprise Danny. The retirement home was located right outside of Aspen, Colorado. With all those affluent people just down the road, it was no wonder they were looking for donations to write off at tax time. What better place than Morning Star?

"It's not the flowers I'm worried about," Danny said, still unable to look away from them. The vase had some roses, daisies, and others he didn't know the names of. "It's the note. Did you not read it?"

His mother scrunched her face as she finally looked away from the TV and met his gaze.

Danny plucked the note off the nightstand, turning it in her direction. "It says Dexter Jordan."

"Dexter Jordan," she repeated, nodding along. Emptiness filled her eyes. The name didn't ring any bells for his mother. Not even close to his reaction upon seeing the name. A name he'd thought about every single day of his life. The name that kept him up late most nights.

"You really don't remember Dexter Jordan?" Danny asked. "Or why this is a big deal?"

Tatiana shrugged and offered a soft smile. "I'm sorry, mijo. I'm trying, but I don't remember."

Dealing with dementia in a parent brought a powerful mixture of rage and grief. The two emotions could intertwine at any moment. Danny had his fair share of blowups when first adjusting to this new normal, but had since learned how to keep himself under control. It wasn't his mom's fault she couldn't remember the simplest details of her past. Hell, it wasn't *anyone's* fault. Perhaps that's what made this so frustrating.

"When did the flowers get dropped off?" Danny asked, the note now crumpled inside of his trembling hand.

"This morning."

"Dammit," Danny muttered under his breath, knowing his mother wouldn't hear it across the room.

They not only knew *where* his mother was, but *when* Danny preferred to visit. They were keeping track. Until now, Danny believed he had kept cool. Moving from state to state, city to city. But none of it mattered.

"What's wrong?" Tatiana asked. "Do you know Dexter Jordan? I thought that was just the name of the person who sent the flowers. Lots of places do that now, you know? I got a tin of cookies around

Christmas time, and it came with a note saying who packed the tin. Really cute."

This wasn't something from the florist. No logo. No explanation. Just the scrawl of the name. The note wasn't intended for his mom.

A calling card from someone trying to get in his head.

"Have you had any strange visitors? Or maybe phone calls?" Danny asked, crumbling the note in his fist. He scanned the room, looking for any signs of hidden cameras or bugs, checking under the lampshade, behind the TV, under the bed. He'd be damned if they pulled a stunt like that on him.

"I'm sorry, Daniel. I'm not remembering anything." His mother tremored and wept at her inability to recall anything of significance.

Seeing his mother cry twisted like a knife in his gut. The image snapped him out of it, the hairs prickling on the back of his neck as though someone from the hallway were watching them.

Danny circled around his mother's bed and dropped to a knee in front of her recliner. He squeezed her shaking hands. "I'm sorry, Ma. Don't be so hard on yourself."

She shook her head. "I know I'm not making life any easier for you. It's so hard for me to remember things. With the names and all the secrets. I just…can't. I'm sorry."

"No, Ma. You have nothing to apologize for. I worry about you is all. If the wrong people ever find out where you're living, I don't know what I'd do. I'd never let myself live it down."

Tatiana wiped her tears away and grabbed Danny's face. "You've always been an emotional boy, and I love that about you. I'm sure that's because you grew up without your father. I always tried my best, mijo, but I could never fill that void. A boy needs his father to show him how to navigate life as a man. It's not fair what happened to us."

Tears rolled down Danny's face. He hadn't heard his mother speak of his father in several months. He thought she'd forgotten all about him. If Armando Cortez had slipped into the void of her memories, just like where she'd placed her keys, could Danny blame her? He'd been dead all of Danny's thirty-six years of life. Had Tatiana forgotten those details? Did she even understand the depth of thirty-six years in her current state?

Danny pulled his mother into an embrace, forcing her to stand up from the recliner. They hugged and swayed for several seconds, crying into each other.

"I worry about *you*," she finally said, pulling back. She looked up at him, her moist brown eyes studying his weathered face. Danny couldn't remember the last time he had gazed into his mother's eyes. Her once thick, brown hair was almost entirely white now. Lines webbed across her face. She had become so frail, no longer the strong woman he'd always admired. "You come in here, paranoid, looking all over the room like someone's hiding. Makes me wonder if you should be the one in this place and not me."

Danny frowned, but his mother broke into a fit of laughter.

"I'm kidding," she said, slapping him across the chest. "You're just like your father. Always on high alert. Always waiting for something to happen. Do you know what I've learned since I've been living here? It's okay to sit and just be. I don't know how many hours I've spent staring out this window. Admiring the nature outside. The world is a beautiful place if you let it be."

Danny looked out the window. The views of the mountains were breathtaking, he couldn't deny that. Deer approached the home multiple times each week, and it always made the residents' day. But Danny saw more than his mother did while looking out the same window. Yes, this little corner of the world might have provided her with the peace she—and he—needed in these final years.

But the world wasn't a beautiful place. Far from it. Not with so many people wanting him buried six feet under.

Tatiana squeezed his hand. "Why don't you sit down and tell me about Dexter Jordan."

DANNY PLACED a call for a Diet Coke for his mother, which she giddily took long gulps from.

"You know Dexter Jordan," he said. "I talk about him every time I come to visit."

Tatiana's eyes flickered, but not with the ferocity he had hoped.

"Oh," she said. "You used to work with him, right?"

Danny kept examining the room, looking for any sign of a recording device. Spotting none, he gradually fell into a state of cautious ease. He sighed as he sat on the edge of his mother's bed after she returned to her recliner. She turned off the TV and gave her son her full attention.

"Dexter," he said, staring at the floor as the shame that so frequently washed over him returned. "Dex. My partner at the DEA. Well, I was more *his* partner. He did all the dirty work in the field. I was just the brains behind everything."

Now Tatiana's eyes lit up, and she clapped a hand to her forehead. "My God! Yes, I remember him now. I'm sorry, mijo. It's all coming back now. Dexter Jordan. Rest his soul."

Danny raised a hand. "We don't know if he's actually dead. It's presumed, but there's no proof. If the cartel has him, there's no saying what they could be making him do."

"Wasn't he killed in the line of duty?" she asked. Her brow furrowed the way it always did when she tried to recall a memory. It's how Danny knew she was rummaging through the messy drawers of her thoughts to find that one thing.

Danny shook his head. "No, Ma. That was Dad. Remember?"

He shuffled toward his mother and dropped to a knee again, this time caressing the hands that rested in her lap. Her bottom lip trembled, but Danny didn't know if she was upset because she couldn't remember how her own husband had died, or if those specific memories had brought back the flood of sorrow.

Tatiana nodded, gazing into the distance. "Right." Her voice wavered. "My husband, Armando Cortez, was killed in Desert Storm on January 18, 1991. You were only eighteen months old when it happened."

"And it's been you and me ever since," Danny added, squeezing his mom's hands. As odd as it was when she'd rattle off details, it still brought Danny comfort knowing she remembered. Tatiana had been so much more than a woman sitting in a retirement home waiting for her mind to slip completely into the void.

She was also a widower. A single mother who'd raised her only son to become the first from her family to graduate from college. She had launched a network of pen pals for her fellow widowers who'd lost their husbands to war, and transitioned to the internet, where emails and message boards replaced the letter writing. Tatiana had worked three jobs while Danny was in high school, all so she could help her son through college at the prestigious University of Denver. She'd never complained and always wore a smile. Even after sixteen hours at work, she'd still make time to spend with Danny, whether it was helping with homework or sitting down to chat about his life.

Tatiana let a single tear roll down her cheek before wiping it away. "I don't know why God put us through hell. But I'm glad I had you by my side."

Danny grinned and patted his mother's hands. "You're my hero, Ma. Don't ever forget it. I still want to be like you when I grow up."

They chuckled at the remark, and Danny returned to his spot on the bed.

"What do you suppose this letter with Dexter's name means?" she asked. "Are we in danger?"

Danny smoothed out the note he had stuffed into his pocket and tossed it on the bed next to him. "I don't know. I'm trying not to jump to conclusions, but I can't see why anyone would have gone to the trouble of writing his name on the card and delivering it with the flowers. Today of all days, like they knew I'd be here to see it." He ran a hand through his wavy hair. "You're sure you haven't seen or spoken to anyone out of the ordinary?"

"Nothing. I may forget many things, but I haven't forgotten the trouble you've gone through to keep me safe. 'My name is Ana Garcia. I never married or had kids. I have one nephew—you—from my sister who passed away in a car accident in 1999. I took in my nephew and raised him as my own.' How was that?"

Danny nodded appreciatively. "Perfection. If anyone ever asks about you or your past, that's all you need to say."

"I practice every day after breakfast," she said. "I read it once, then recite it in my head, then in a whisper so no one can hear."

Danny had written that exact script on a notecard and tucked it into his mother's Bible in her nightstand drawer. He hated worrying her, but she understood the gravity of those who might be after him and what that could mean for her.

"So, my Armando was killed in Desert Storm," she said. "But I can't remember what happened to Dexter. You say he's not dead?"

Danny shrugged. "I like to believe he's alive and will return to his family one day. I just need to find him."

"The world is a big place, mijo. Don't stress yourself trying to find the needle in a haystack."

Danny sighed. All he did was stress himself out. The past tore at him like a vulture feasting on roadkill. He had too many wrongs to right, but none as pressing as finding his old partner.

"Dex is gone because of me. We were working on a mission in New Mexico. I was doing surveillance and scouting the area before his arrival. I saw nothing, so I gave him the green light to get out of his hideout and drive toward our destination."

"Then it's not really your fault," his mother said.

Danny looked down at his fidgeting fingers, ignoring the comment. "The cartel was hiding. They knew we were coming and knew the exact blind spots to get around my surveillance. It was an ambush. They grabbed him, ripped him out of the car, and threw him in the dirt. All I could do was watch. It was just me hiding in my van with nothing but a pistol."

"You had to save yourself. No one can blame you for that."

"There were eight of them—I never had a chance. They kicked him, spit on him, made his face completely unrecognizable. But I never saw them kill him. No guns were fired as they dragged him away. And once they did, a trio of those men started toward me. Hopped in a truck and crashed into my van. I had never fired my service pistol outside the shooting range, but I had no choice. So I rolled out of the van and started firing."

Danny's body tensed, both hands balled into fists. It was his mother's turn to rise from the recliner and embrace her son. His body shivered against her chest. Unclenching his jaw took a focused effort. Tatiana stroked the back of his head.

"Let it out, mijo," she said. "You can't hold this in forever."

"I killed a man that day, Ma. First time. I'll never forget it. My bullet tore right through his chest. A bullseye on his heart. We locked eyes as he fell to the ground and bled out. That's when I got shot in the ear."

Danny reached up and rubbed the jagged groove on his left ear. The cartel had fired back and missed by that much.

"You're here, son," she said, placing a firm hand on his chest. "Breathing. Alive and well. You have so much life ahead of you. I just wish you could see that."

His mother's words barely reached the edge of his conscious thoughts. All he could picture was that evening in the desert. The stench of blood and death filling the air. Burned rubber from the truck that had sped toward his van. He'd kept shooting, killed another one of them. That's when the third had gotten back in the truck to speed away. He could have killed him, too, but his arms had turned to mush by that point.

"I pray for you every night," Tatiana said. "It was kill or be killed. You'll be forgiven."

She had raised Danny as Catholic, but he had struggled with his faith ever since that evening. He no longer believed in God or an afterlife. Hell was on Earth, not some underground lair set on fire.

Even so, he appreciated his mother's prayers. It was her way of coping with the madness.

If there was a God, then Dexter would be out there. Somewhere. Waiting to hug his wife and two sons again.

That was the only reminder he needed of his purpose in this world. Danny pulled away from his mother and turned for the door.

"I'll be right back, Ma. I need to make a phone call."

CHAPTER
THREE

THE PHONE RANG while Danny paced circles in the courtyard outside the retirement home. He beat himself up for not remembering the only other person who knew where his mother was. It had to be her fault.

The weather was warm for an April afternoon in Aspen. A handful of the residents wore light jackets to enjoy chess and dominoes at the outdoor tables. A couple watched Danny as he stared at the ground, urging the phone to be answered.

"Hello, Daniel," a woman's stern voice greeted.

"Nadia," Danny replied. "Who have you been talking to? Someone knows where my mom is living."

"Excuse you," Nadia fired back, matching Danny's rage. "You have some nerve. Calling me after all these months. Not so much as a hello before spewing out false accusations."

"What am I supposed to think?" Danny returned the glare of an elderly man at the chess table. *Maybe worry about moving your knight and leave me alone.* "Besides my mother and me, you're the only soul in the world who knows where she's staying."

"Why don't you back up, asshole? And actually tell me what's going on."

Danny sighed. He immediately regretted the phone call. But it had to be done. He and Nadia had once shared a life together. Their passion had been as electric as this conversation. He wondered, on all his lonely nights, how his life might have looked had he followed Nadia to Chicago. He had refused, citing his bright future with the DEA. And saw it flushed away a few months later with nothing to show for it except for a heart full of regret.

"Fine," Danny said. "I arrived at my mom's about an hour ago. She had a vase of flowers on her nightstand. Delivered earlier this morning. A note accompanying them. Handwritten. All it said was *Dexter Jordan*."

Danny let his words linger a moment. After ten seconds without a response, he called out, "Nadia, are you there?"

"I'm here," she said flatly. "Just thinking."

Danny pursed his lips and continued his frantic pacing.

After another minute, Nadia said, "Sorry, Danny. It wasn't me. I try not to even think about your mother, for fear of letting something slip." Nadia lowered her voice. "It's the cost of faking someone's death, you know?"

The words smacked Danny across the face. He had fallen into such a routine of visiting and calling his mother that he often forgot the trouble Nadia had gone through to falsify the death of Tatiana Cortez.

As far as the public believed, Tatiana had died peacefully in her sleep after battling cancer for a year. The reason Nadia had moved to Chicago was for a job in the Attorney General's office. Combined with her uncanny ability to negotiate and influence people, Nadia had gained access to the all the documents needed to arrange the ruse. She'd overseen all the details, right down to the obituary that was published online.

"What am I supposed to do?" Danny dropped onto a vacant bench overlooking a dry stone fountain.

"What does your gut say?" Nadia asked, her voice switching to one of comfort.

Danny drew in a long breath and blew it out. "My gut says we've been found out. I have a hard time believing this is some wild coincidence."

"It is April Fool's Day," Nadia said. "You don't think someone's playing a really sick joke, do you?"

"I wish that was all. But no one's laughing. If they know where she lives, then they probably know where I'm living, too. I don't mind sleeping with a gun under my pillow, but I can't ask my mom to do that."

"Then we need to move her," Nadia said. "As soon as possible."

Nadia and Tatiana had developed a strong relationship when Nadia had dated Danny. Nadia came from a broken family and considered Tatiana a second mother. They'd go shopping together, watch chick flicks, and even crochet while swapping life stories. Danny never had to doubt Nadia's interest in protecting his mother. He shouldn't have accused her of letting the location slip.

"Are you able to help?" Danny asked. "We discussed if this were to happen, I would have to lie low. Definitely can't come see my mom, in case someone's following me."

"I know. I can't take time off for at least a couple of days but I can get out there next week. I'll start the paperwork for moving her to a new location, but even that doesn't guarantee when I'll hear back. You want me to use the money from your mom's investment accounts?"

"Yes," Danny said. "That's what it's for."

"Okay, I'll see what I can do. Keep your phone handy."

"Thanks, Nadia. I'm not sure where I'll be, but I'll stay within an eight-hour drive from Aspen."

"I don't like when you go into hiding, Danny."

"I don't exactly have a choice right now."

She was silent for a moment. "You think it's them, don't you?"

Danny gulped down the ball of saliva that had formed in his mouth. "I always plan for the worst-case scenario. If it's them, then I'm fully prepared. If not, then I'm overly prepared."

"It can be anyone, Danny," she said. "You testified in how many trials that resulted in convictions?"

"Too many. I was good at my job, but Dex was even better. I was just the boring expert giving testimony to cover our bases. No one out there should want me except for the cartel who took Dex."

"You don't sound as distraught as I'd expect," Nadia said.

"All my worry is for my mom right now. I'll be fine. In fact, I have some hope now."

"Hope?"

Danny nodded. "Of course. Why would the cartel go through all this trouble of delivering this message to me if Dex wasn't still alive?"

"Because you killed two of their own, and they don't let those things go. Plus, their boss is in prison because of you. He's still calling the shots. I deal with plenty of organized crime here in Chicago, and these people are ruthless, Danny. You need to be careful. They're as vicious with mental and emotional warfare as they are with their guns and explosives. I'm glad you're feeling some hope, but you have to remind yourself this could all be a ploy to ambush you."

"They'll never get me again," Danny said. "Over my dead body."

"And that's all they want."

"I still have a contact with the DEA. He's promised to let me know if there's anything I need to worry about."

"I know that. Has he called you?" Nadia asked.

"Not yet. Maybe I'll reach out to him just to check in. Always good to have an extra set of eyes watching my back."

Nadia sighed. "Just promise me you won't do anything stupid. Your mom still needs you. And I'll need your help, Danny. At least with explaining what's going on and why she's moving."

And I need you, Danny thought, not daring to utter those words aloud. Even with how the phone call had started, Danny still longed for Nadia and the life he let slip through his fingers.

He'd never close the door on a potential second chance with her. That was the main reason he never confessed his feelings. If he did, that opened him to a response from Nadia. And if she didn't feel the same, he wasn't sure he could handle that truth. The door would close forever. All a man needed was a sliver of hope to keep moving, even if it was misguided. Even if deep down, his heart already knew the truth.

Danny blocked out the doubt as he marched on, hoping for a chance at redemption in multiple facets of his life.

"I'll be fine." Danny squeezed the cell phone until his knuckles turned white. Just when he had thought his life was getting into a routine—at least for him—he had to deal with this. "Thanks again for your help. I can't tell you how much I appreciate it. Sorry for how I started the call."

Tell her you love her. Just like all those years ago. Back when we were in love. Together. As a team.

But he didn't utter those three words. Not now.

"You're welcome, Danny," Nadia said. "Be careful out there. I'll be thinking of you."

CHAPTER
FOUR

DANNY RETURNED to his motel room at the Motor Owl Lodge twenty minutes north of Aspen. He always stayed at the same place for his monthly visits and wondered if this would be his last time in the trucker motel right off I-70. Danny wished he could vary the timing of his visits, but having set dates made it easier on his mother's dementia.

He had no home to call his own, but often relaxed at his mother's house in Denver, happy to bounce around from hotel to hotel when hiding across the country. Danny was in hot water now and wouldn't dare drive by his mom's house. Not until things cooled off.

His room reeked of cigarette and marijuana smoke. The walls might as well have been paper. He heard snoring and blaring televisions as he flicked on the light switch. Having checked in last night, Danny's belongings lay scattered about the room. A backpack, laptop, water bottle, a container of weed, and a Glock 17.

He had started smoking the reefer shortly after leaving the DEA. It was the only thing that helped ease his PTSD. Plus, it numbed the pain of losing Dexter. The pain of his best friend's death hadn't really waned, and he supposed it wouldn't until justice was delivered. The tragedy had sent his life on a new trajectory, one he no longer knew the final destination.

Most of Danny's nights alone centered on smoking a bowl and playing poker online. He'd picked up that habit after Nadia moved away. He'd played at least three times a week since.

He grabbed his pipe and lighter from the nightstand and let the smoke fill his lungs. One or two hits was all he needed to feel at ease but not catch a high.

Stashing the pipe away, Danny crossed the room and sat down at the desk facing the wall with heavy snoring. He flipped open his laptop and powered it on, leaning to his right to grab the television remote.

The TV was more for background noise and opened to a Taco Bell commercial. Once the old laptop was warmed up, Danny opened the PokerKing software and examined a list of upcoming tournaments. Entry fees ranged anywhere from fifty cents to five thousand dollars. He preferred playing events around thirty dollars and joined the first tournament he spotted at that price. It wouldn't start for another fifteen minutes, so he opened a map to study the areas he and Nadia had long-ago discussed for relocating his mother.

Salt Lake City. Cheyenne. Omaha. Des Moines. Chicago.

None of these cities were too far from Denver. His 2014 Toyota Tundra was already pushing 150,000 miles but had never given him issues. Driving to Salt Lake in the winter could be challenging, especially if they closed the tunnels in the Rockies. He'd push for Cheyenne or Omaha when the time came.

Chicago could be convenient since Nadia lived there.

Danny pulled out his cell phone to call Nadia, pulled up her number, and stared at the phone. He quickly tossed it behind him on the bed.

Estupido!

He couldn't expect her to look after his mother. Sometimes the weed made him *too* loose and overconfident.

The commercial break ended, and the programming returned to the evening news. Danny checked the countdown timer on his computer screen, which showed another thirteen minutes until the tournament started.

The news anchor chatted about an upcoming festival in downtown Aspen, droning on about vendors, performers, and a complete list of things Danny didn't care about. Then an alert chimed and prompted Danny to look over at the TV.

BREAKING NEWS! flashed across the screen in a quick graphic before returning to the anchor, a young woman with curly brown hair who Danny had always hoped to bump into one of these days while in Aspen. Her name was Jasmine McCoy, and she still had no ring on any of her fingers.

"Breaking news from Florence, Colorado." Jasmine batted her green eyes at the camera, melting hearts all across the Western Slope. "Mexican drug lord Victor Villa, who was serving a life sentence in ADX Florence, has escaped from prison. Officials gave no details on the means of his escape."

"What?!" Danny jumped out of his seat and stood in front of the TV, eyes wide as he stared at the old mugshot of the man he'd put behind bars. Villa had his black hair buzzed, a pointy nose, and dark eyes with no sign of life swimming behind them.

"Villa recently suffered a broken shoulder from an incident in the prison and was staying in the medical ward at the time of his escape. Prison officials are investigating whether Villa had accomplices on the inside or if he merely seized a spur-of-the-moment opportunity. He is considered dangerous and should not be approached. If spotted, call 9-1-1 immediately."

"This isn't happening," Danny said to the TV. His stomach flipped in cartwheels. That mug shot lingered a moment longer, Villa's gaze locking with Danny's through the screen.

It all made sense. This had to be an orchestrated escape. The cartel Villa led, Los Leones, had no shortage of resources—unlimited money and thousands of people. That combination could get Villa out of the harshest of prisons. Like ADX Florence.

The note arrived at his mother's retirement home on the same day that Villa escaped from prison. Danny didn't believe in coincidences. Not when the cartel was involved.

The news coverage quickly shifted to the weather, so Danny returned to his computer to search for more about Villa.

The *Denver Post* had published an article ten minutes earlier, discussing the reign of terror Victor Villa once led. Responsible for over 10,000 deaths across Mexico and the United States. Smuggler of weapons, cocaine, heroin, and meth. The journalist had no details regarding the escape, aside from information that the convict was reported missing at exactly 5:03 PM.

A manhunt was underway. The nearest airport to the prison, a ten-minute drive north in Fremont, was ordered to ground all flights and lockdown their small facility. FBI and DEA agents were en route to Florence and nearby Cañon City to begin their searches of the area.

The prison was strategically located in the middle of the mountains to make an escape by foot incredibly difficult. One would need to be in excellent shape to hike through the mountains. And with a broken shoulder, Villa had no chance.

Danny clicked through more articles, finding nothing of significance. He even checked the Mexican news websites where the story had yet to break.

Danny finally landed on Villa's Wikipedia page, where he read about his previous history of violence and corruption. And, of course, the trial where he received two life sentences.

A trial Danny could close his eyes and transport himself back to.

He had taken the witness stand against Villa, explaining how his job as a DEA Intelligence Research Specialist helped lead to locating Villa and his eventual capture. The trial had run two months, but Danny and Dexter both attended the day of the verdict reading.

After the judge had completed reading the guilty verdicts for all thirty-nine counts, Villa calmly turned to face the audience and jury.

"I will see you all again one day." He had grinned, revealing yellowed teeth. "And you will all pay."

Villa had spoken with such confidence that Danny believed him. And while the drug lord's eyes looked over everyone in the gallery, his stare only locked with a handful of people.

Danny was one of them.

"He's coming for me," Danny whispered. He opened his poker tournament and promptly withdrew, getting his money back before the game started.

As much as he worried about his mother, he now had to figure how he'd navigate life with Villa on the run. It could be a few days, maybe weeks, before Villa would land on his feet and return to calling the shots. But Danny was on the short list of people for whom Villa thirsted for revenge.

There was one thing Danny had learned about Villa during his many months studying the drug lord from afar. If Villa wanted you dead, then you'd be hunted down and murdered. Even in broad daylight, if that's what it took.

Danny needed to move his mother, then himself. He might just ask Nadia to handle the moving of his mom and not tell him where she was staying. Not knowing where his mother would be would certainly lead to sleepless nights. But her safety was more important than Danny's REM cycles. The less he knew, the better. Just in case.

Heart racing, sweat trickling down the sides of his face, he grabbed his phone and dialed Nadia, hoping it wasn't already too late.

CHAPTER
FIVE

NADIA ANSWERED, panting for breath.

"Did I interrupt something?" Danny chuckled. He sat on the foot of his bed, glaring at the marijuana pipe on the desk next to his laptop.

"I was just running on the treadmill," she replied through long gasps, returning to normal after a few seconds. "Why are you calling me so soon? I haven't heard anything back from the homes yet."

"Have you heard the news?"

"I haven't been on my phone or near a TV for the last couple hours. What's going on?"

"Victor Villa has escaped from prison."

Danny let those words linger in the airwaves between them.

"Hold on," Nadia said, a loud ruffling noise followed by the sound of her finger tapping on her phone's screen. "My God, Danny."

"You didn't believe me?"

"Of course I did. That's just one of those things you need to see for yourself. How the hell could he have escaped from that prison? Isn't it supposed to be one of the most secure in the country?"

"It *is* the most secure. That's why I'm thinking it was an inside job."

"That's a loaded theory."

"Is it? That prison has been deemed 'escape proof.' The inmates have zero contact with each other, so Villa couldn't have plotted something with another prisoner. He spends twenty-three hours each day locked in a seven-by-twelve cell with steel walls. No windows to the outside world. His one hour of outdoor time is alone with a half-dozen guards watching his every move. I suspect his move to the infirmary played a role in his escape."

"No way the staff there could be influenced into helping," she replied. "Those positions are so heavily vetted."

"Anyone can be bought." Danny bit his bottom lip as he recounted Villa offering Dexter ten million dollars to be set free. Dexter had added bribery to the charges. "All it takes is one person to take the bait. Villa is a con man and sweet talker. I'm sure he's been trying all these years to find the right person. I'm dying to know how he broke his shoulder. All the news says is there was an incident."

"If he doesn't encounter other inmates, then a guard could have hurt him."

"Or he did it himself." Danny rubbed his eyes. "I spent months studying this man. He's unbelievably smart. Broken shoulder followed shortly by his escape? It has to be an inside job."

Nadia sighed. "So, what does this mean for you?"

"It means I'm in serious trouble."

"I know that, Danny. What's your next move?"

"That's why I called." Danny had muted the TV and now paced back and forth in front of it, something he'd always done when on the phone. "I need to go to New Mexico. First thing in the morning."

"What's in New Mexico?" she asked. "Hasn't that state taken enough from you?"

"It's where Villa's going. I'm sure of it."

"And you're wanting to…what? Say hello? Why on earth would you go where he's going?"

"I need to find out everything I can about Dex. Villa will know."

Nadia let out an anxious laugh. "Danny, are you even listening to yourself? Victor Villa wants you dead! If you walk up to him, he'll shoot you without a word."

"He won't. Has too much of an ego. Likes to play the psychological game. I studied him, remember?"

"How can I forget? It's all you talked about at the dinner table for eighteen months. Hell, I could probably recite all the facts you know about Villa."

Danny chuckled. "Sorry about that. I wish I had done so many things differently. But you know how it is."

Nadia's voice softened. "Sadly, I do. It's the same for us attorneys. Obsessing over clients, files, details. If we had dinner tonight, I'd be talking your ear off about the money laundering case I've been working on for the past three months."

"Riveting." Danny smiled, wishing he *could* have dinner with Nadia.

"You're calling me for a favor," she said, "so just spit it out."

Apparently, Nadia wasn't experiencing the same longing for Danny's company.

"I don't want to know where my mom is going. Are you able to handle everything on your own?"

"Jesus, Danny."

"I know, but hear me out. I trust nothing right now. How long until these guys bug my phone? Email, snail mail, it doesn't matter. I can't trust any line of communication. If anything gets intercepted by these goons, then my mother might as well sit in her living room at home and wait for them to come."

The other end of the line remained silent for long seconds, but Danny heard the beeping from the treadmill in the background.

Give her time to think.

"Okay," she finally said. "I can move some things around and will fly out the day after tomorrow. I'll take your mom somewhere safe while we finalize her next living situation."

"Thank you."

"I'm not done." Nadia's tone caught Danny off guard, causing him to plop down at the foot of the bed. "I have terms."

"Name them."

"I'm only doing this as a favor to your mother. Not you. Understood?"

"Yes, ma'am."

"Good. And I'm going to need some sort of notification that you're okay. Doesn't need to be daily. How about weekly? Find a pay phone or get a new burner phone—it doesn't matter to me— but call my *office* once a week. Do *not* call my cell. If you're right, and these guys are following you, I can't have them knowing who I am."

"And why do you need to hear from me?"

"Really, Danny? You're the one opting to play with fire. I've been telling you for years to take your mom and move to an island. Or Europe. Just go away somewhere these people won't find you. But here you are, planning to knock on the door of a man who wants to kill you. And for what, I'm not even sure."

"For Dex," Danny said. "For his wife and kids. They deserve to know the truth and get closure. You can't talk me out of it."

Nadia snorted. "Oh, that ship has long since sailed. If you cared what anyone had to say, this conversation wouldn't be happening. You're stubborn beyond belief."

The words hurt Danny, but he couldn't dwell on them. As much as he'd tried working on himself and improving his character, Danny could never stray from his foundation. Having grown up as the man of the house, he'd shouldered more decision-making than he should have as a child. Which had led to him having control problems as an adult.

"I need you to check in weekly just to know you're alive," Nadia said. "Nothing more. Nothing less. If you die, I need to inform your mother. I refuse to feed her any lies about what you're doing. I assume you have?"

"I haven't told her about any of this, and I'm not going to. Before I leave in the morning, I'll call and tell her you'll be in touch soon. I'll visit as soon as I'm able."

Nadia was silent for a moment. "This is all so wrong, Danny. Your mother's had a hard life, and you just keep dragging her through the mud because *you* can't make the right decisions."

Danny gritted his teeth. "You don't know the half of what we've been through together, so I suggest you shut your mouth."

"There he is. Don't anybody give Danny Cortez advice. If it's something he doesn't want to hear, you'll be cast out as the enemy."

Danny balled his free hand into a fist, fingernails digging into his palm. "The only thing that has kept me going is knowing I still need to find out what happened to Dex."

"He's dead, Danny. For the love of God, come to terms with that. You're going to get yourself killed trying to find a dead man. You're obsessed. Let him go."

"Easy for you to say. You've never even lost someone close to you. Your parents are alive. Two grandparents passed *before* you were born, and the other two are still swinging golf clubs in Arizona. Have you ever even been to a funeral?"

Danny couldn't help himself in this fit of anger. Speaking with Nadia sparked a swirl of buried emotions. His heartrate had run high since she answered. He expected her to make matters better, but the opposite stared Danny in the face.

"I know you're dealing with a lot right now," Nadia replied calmly. "So I'm going to let that slide. Just stay in touch, okay? Hopefully, that's not too much of a burden for you while I'm making sure *your* mother stays safe."

The reality of the words he'd just spewed circled back and

smacked him in the head. How could he expect her to give him a second chance if all they did was trade verbal barbs?

"I'm sorry, Nadia. Thank you for everything. I'll be in touch."

CHAPTER
SIX

DANNY WOKE before the sun rose, gathered his belonging, and drove east.

His backpack sat on the passenger seat while he cruised on I-70. He'd called his mother and let her know Nadia would help her get moved to a new location.

Why? He couldn't say. Only that her safety was his top priority, and staying in Aspen was no longer safe.

He kept the phone call short and sweet, promising to call her back as soon as possible.

With a four-hour drive to Denver, Danny stopped in Breckenridge, roughly halfway, for breakfast at a local diner. The town was quiet, with only a handful of people in the diner tending to their steaming mugs of coffee. He had cut back on his coffee intake since leaving the DEA. Today, he'd make an exception.

Taking a corner table for privacy, Danny pulled out his cell phone and scrolled through his contacts until finding Zakary Larocque. He'd debated calling him ever since he'd found the note on his mother's nightstand. A desperate move, even knowing Zakary wouldn't take it that way.

"Nothing to lose," Danny said, and dialed his old friend.

"Is this who I think it is?" Zakary answered.

"Still don't trust caller ID?" Danny grinned. "Zak, how the hell are you?"

Zak laughed and slapped the surface of his desk. "Danny Cortez. Real quick, though. Can I call you back on this same number?"

"Not a problem."

"Give me one minute."

The call disconnected, and Danny stared at his phone. Forty seconds later, it rang from a different number.

"Zak?" he answered. "Everything okay?"

"It is now," his old friend said. "Rather be safe than sorry. Got a burner phone just for calls with you."

"Still that bad at the office?"

"Let's just say everyone is being watched. Scrutiny is through the roof. Privacy out the door." Zak lowered his voice. "I've been expecting your call."

"Is that right?"

"Of course. Victor Villa has escaped from prison. Who else would I have thought of after hearing the news? Just you." Zak cleared his throat and softened his voice. "And Dex."

"It's fine," Danny said. "That's why I'm calling, actually."

"I also heard from Nadia late last night."

Danny rubbed his forehead. "Nadia called you?"

"Sure did. We had a long talk catching up. Things are going really well for her in Chicago."

Danny bit his bottom lip, forcing out his next words. "Yes. Good for her."

"I'm sure you know all about it. But she didn't want to talk about her. She called to tell me about you. Not doing too well right now, are you?"

Danny and Zak had formed a strong friendship at the DEA. Both were straight shooters who never beat around the bush. Both had bright futures in the agency. But only one remained.

"I've had better days," Danny said. The server brought him his coffee, and he quickly pointed at the French toast and eggs on the menu.

"I'm sure," Zak said. "Sounds like nothing's going your way right now."

"Why did she call you?"

"Just worried about you. Says you're not thinking straight and are in way over your head. Are you really going to New Mexico to see Villa?"

"That's the plan." Danny blew a breath through flared nostrils. "I wish everyone would stop making it sound like I'm going there to ring his doorbell and have a fun chat over a couple of beers. I know stealth."

"At least you know that much. Personally, I think you're being reckless. Dex is dead. I know you hate hearing it, but the statistics suggest that's the only outcome. It's been two years, Danny. I loved Dex as much as you, but it's time to let him go. There's nothing we can do about it."

Hearing these words from someone who knew Dexter as well as Danny made things more real. But he didn't have to accept it. Not yet.

"Look, Zak, I'm doing this. And there's nothing anyone can say to stop me." He fiddled with the drink napkin, folding it into halves then quarters. "I was hoping you could help me. Are you still working in intelligence?"

"Senior Director." Zak cackled. "Can you believe it? They put me in *charge* of intelligence."

Zak had long joked he would one day run the entire DEA. He was well on his way. "Good for you, man. I'm happy for you."

"Thank you. As for Villa, we've already got people looking into it. New Mexico seems the best bet for where he's headed."

"You ever get any of his other guys?" Danny asked. He had helped capture Villa and deliver his justice, but they'd never caught anyone else from his cartel. Dex had tried bargaining with the drug lord, going as far as offering immunity if he turned in every single person from his criminal organization. Villa had responded by spitting on Dex's face.

"Afraid not," Zak said. "We know where they are. Most are in New Mexico, but a few have spread out to Arizona and West Texas."

"If you know where they are, why haven't you made a move?"

"Too much risk. After what happened to you and Dex, they won't approve a raid in such a remote location. Not without having more boots on the ground—which has been the actual struggle. We're outgunned. Tried seeing if the National Guard could help, but the governor won't cooperate. Says New Mexican lives are safe right now. No need to stir up a situation that could result in the loss of innocent lives."

"That's insanity."

"I know. But that's how cartels take over cities. If you don't squash them like the bugs they are, as soon as they roll in, they just keep multiplying." Zak sighed. "I really hope the governor will change his mind before it's too late. We're trying everything we can from out here, but Steele has been keeping a tight grip on all decisions."

Danny rolled his eyes at the name. Chuck Steele, as he was known around the offices, served as the DEA Deputy Administrator, one spot away from overseeing the department.

"Steele," Danny repeated. "Still out there raising hell for everyone?"

"Forever and always. He came in this morning pretty fired up about the Villa news. Says we need all hands on deck to capture him. Pulling agents off assignments to re-direct them. Had a talk with me about using Intelligence to pinpoint the routes Villa might use to escape Colorado. He's not entirely sold on him returning to New Mexico and wants us to enforce checkpoints at all states bordering Colorado. That's seven states! We're already understaffed in the field."

"Why doesn't he use his contacts on Capitol Hill to get that measure approved?"

Steele was never shy to name drop the congressmen or senators he had dinner with, always framing it as something he did in the best interest of the DEA. He even had the audacity to email blast the entire office with a picture of himself meeting the vice president in the Oval Office.

"Oh, he wants to," Zak said. "But he's holding off for now. The Senate is going through a leadership change. Plus, there are talks of him finally getting his shot to run the department. He doesn't want to ruffle any feathers in the Senate right now."

"Mildred is stepping down?" Danny had enjoyed half his cup of coffee before putting it back on the table. Alice Mildred served as the current DEA Administrator.

"There are talks. She might get a cabinet position in the White House. But you know how rumors are in D.C."

"If that's true, God help the DEA if Steele takes the reins."

"I try to not think about it and just focus on my job." Zak paused, and Danny heard the scratching of a pen on paper. "Tell you what, let me do some digging on Villa and see what I can find."

"How long do you think?"

"Could be a few weeks. Like I said, Steele is moving all kinds of things around. I think he's being rather short in his decision-making, but who am I to tell him?"

Danny tossed his free hand in the air. "And that all started this morning?"

"I wish. He's been like this for the past month. Never seen anything like it here. Some of our field agents are months deep into assignments, and he's pulling them off, assigning them to other cases. It's creating a ton of tension in the office."

"Is he breaking up teams?"

As an intelligence analyst, Danny worked with a select few field agents on their missions. That's what led to him meeting Dexter and eventually working with him exclusively. The department had always made a point to keep teams and partners the same, only changing them if absolutely necessary.

"He is. And people aren't happy. They need continuity in who they're working with and feel that Steele is just yanking the rug out from under them. I don't hear as much on the floor now that I'm a director—conversations stop when I walk by, it's kind of funny—but the consensus is that everyone in the office is fed up with Steele."

"And nothing from Mildred?"

"She's not involved in all the day-to-day. Steele really shouldn't be, either, but you know how he is."

Yeah, a control freak.

"I gotta run, Danny," Zak said. "Speak of the devil. I'll call you if I learn anything."

"Thanks, Zak. Talk soon."

They hung up, and a feeling kept gnawing at Danny's gut. By the time the server returned with his plate of food, Danny had lost his appetite.

Chaos was unfolding in the DEA, but Danny could only afford to worry about himself. Did he really need to pursue Villa on his own if so much effort was already going into capturing the escaped convict?

They weren't interested in finding the truth about Dexter. He'd long been an afterthought. They just needed to get their guy and lock him up again. The cartel would retaliate. They always did. But Danny would be ready for them this time.

I need to visit one more person before I leave for New Mexico.

CHAPTER
SEVEN

DANNY COULDN'T REMEMBER the last time he'd visited his father's gravestone.

Probably seven years, if he had to guess, but maybe longer.

He was only a baby when Armando Cortez was killed in combat during Desert Storm, so he lacked any memories of the man. It made the grief different. No thoughts of his father rushed through his mind, only pictures he had seen over the years. Some showed a smiling man with plenty of joy in his life. Others revealed the stoic nature of the soldier who had given his life for the country he loved.

Growing up without a father had provided plenty of challenges for young Danny, especially once he reached his adolescent years. His mother couldn't teach him how to shave or handle his changing body. But she'd taught him how to throw a baseball and tie a tie. Everything about the gentleman he'd become was thanks to his mother.

Still, an emptiness remained, lingering in Danny's chest throughout his entire life. All he had were stories. His father was quick-witted. Determined. Always strived for more in life. Danny couldn't help but credit his father for passing these intangibles on to him, assuming that was how things worked. It made him feel closer to the father he'd never truly known.

He pulled into Fort Logan National Cemetery on the west side of Denver, precisely five hours after leaving Aspen earlier that morning. The drive had started gray and cloudy, but the sun clawed its way through, casting a magnificent glow over the city.

Thousands of marble headstones lined the cemetery as far as he could see. Thanks to visiting biweekly with his mother during his youth, he had learned the exact route to his father's grave.

When he parked the truck and jumped out, Danny stumbled as he cut through the grass toward his dad's gravestone. His legs became wet noodles, barely supporting him as he trudged forward.

When he reached Armando Cortez, Danny dropped to his knees in the wet grass. His father's name stared at him, teasing him with a lifetime of unknown memories.

"Hi, Dad." Danny held back the rush of tears. "It's me. I'm torn right now. Have no idea what to do. Mom is safe, but I'm not. I can't help thinking I might die in the next few weeks. I'm not sure how you felt going into the war facing the same possibility, but surprisingly, I don't feel all that scared about it."

A flock of geese landed fifty yards away, picking at grass that hadn't quite turned green in these early days of spring.

"I know one way or another, I'm going to get the closure I need. At least about Dex. His situation is my fault, and I have to make it right. That's my only regret. I have plenty of wishes, sure. Wish I could have grown up with you in my life. I think you'd be proud. Fear is always in the back of my mind, though. Fear I might leave a family behind. Or Mom."

A group of mourners marched through the grass across the field, stopping about thirty headstones away from Danny. An older couple with their grandchildren. The kids each held a flower, and the couple had their arms around each other as they looked down at the grave.

"I don't know how heaven works—if it's even a real place. If it is, I hope you'll be waiting for me the day I arrive. There are so many things I want to ask you. And if it's not real, I guess that won't be so bad, either. Just darkness and silence. Sounds nice after life in this chaotic world.

"I'm not sure what I was hoping to get out of visiting you. Maybe a sign. I don't *have* to go to New Mexico. I could just as easily take Mom to an island like Nadia keeps telling me to. But that would mean leaving Nadia for good, and that's not something I want to close the door on. I don't know what she'd want with damaged goods like me, but she still sticks around." Danny's chest tightened. The crossroads of his decision circled him like a predator ready to pounce. "Mom always told me timing is half the battle in life. You can be in the right place at the wrong time. Or you might even be in the wrong place at the right time. It never made a lot of sense to me, but maybe now I'm starting to understand."

The geese flew away, their shadows covering Danny for a quick second as they ventured to the next field. A single robin swooped down from the nearby trees, landing on the gravestone next to Armando's, belonging to John Cortland.

"All I want is to make the world a better place," Danny said, "and right now, that means getting Dex's family the answers they deserve. It's the least I can do, and also the most I can do. I'm well aware of the odds of Dex being alive, but until I have proof, I have to assume there is still something I can do. I've been through so much darkness. What's a little more?"

The robin hopped off the neighboring gravestone and dug in the grass for a worm.

"I'm not too worried about Mom if I get killed. She's in such a decline, I'm not sure how much longer she'll even know my name. She's already forgetting you."

Saying this brought the tears to the forefront, and a lone one made its way down Danny's cheek.

If his mother no longer remembered his father, then who

would? The stories would end—they mostly already had. Armando had some distant cousins in Mexico, but no one who could share anything substantial.

"My life is at a crossroads. Again. I made the wrong decision leaving the DEA when I did. I clearly made the worst decision of my life by letting Nadia go. All I had to do was follow her. The DEA has an office in Chicago. It wouldn't have been any trouble to request a transfer and take a new job."

Danny clenched his jaw. He hated revisiting his past, but sometimes a man needed to do just that. For perspective and clarity. And to understand why he'd ended up here, talking to a marble slab as he contemplated a choice between a suicide mission in New Mexico or life on a beach in the Caribbean.

"I know what I want to do, what I need to do, and what I *should* do. None of them are the same options. I wish you were here to at least share your wisdom. The universe is tugging me toward New Mexico. It doesn't matter where I move in the world, I'll never be able to live with myself until I can close this case for Dex. And now Villa's out. He took my friend and probably killed him. I have the skills to remove him from the world. Even if I don't need to, shouldn't I?"

The robin took cautious steps toward Danny, staring at him. Danny glanced at the bird, wondering if his father was trying to speak to him through the little creature.

"What do you think?"

The robin tweeted and flew on top of Armando's gravestone.

"I must be going crazy." Danny laughed and shook his head. "Out here talking to a bird. That's how I know it's time for me to go."

The family visiting their lost relative nearby remained huddled around the grave, and others started trickling into the cemetery.

It was shortly after noon, and with a six-hour drive to Albuquerque, Danny could make it there by dinner time.

The robin tweeted once more and flew off. South.

That was the only sign Danny needed to confirm his decision. He kissed his fingers and pressed them against the gravestone.

"I'll see you soon, Dad. I love you."

CHAPTER
EIGHT

DANNY WOKE UP IN CATALINA, New Mexico, shortly before noon the next day. Feeling rested after a grueling twelve hours on the road, Danny rolled out of bed, stretched his limbs, and dressed for the day ahead.

He had driven all evening after leaving the cemetery, having planned to stay a night in Albuquerque. But once he'd reached Albuquerque, the motivation to keep going was already boiling over. Just driving through the southwestern desert reminded him of the good times he and Dex had shared in the months leading up to his eventual kidnapping.

The thought of Dexter kept him going. After grabbing a quick bite in ABQ, Danny drove on to Catalina, where he and Dex had stayed prior to the mission that had changed both of their lives.

Catalina was a small town with a population of just under five thousand. It contained a couple hotel chains, a nearby golf course, and a handful of museums. Danny and Dex had always enjoyed blowing off steam while out on assignment and visited the museums if the weather didn't cooperate for a round of golf.

The small town was a prime location for the cartel. Ten minutes from the closest city of Las Cruces. Only ninety from the Mexican border. Most importantly, the cartel's compound sat two hours east in the middle of the desert. The only way to reach it was by knowing the specific dirt roads to take.

The DEA had always talked about demolishing the compound after Villa's capture, but never secured the funding. After Dexter's kidnapping, the department had launched a raid on the compound, finding the place abandoned. They no longer needed to pursue its demolition, despite Danny's desperate pleas to the contrary.

And so it remained. Fully functioning and ready to welcome back any of the cartel's friends. Danny knew the route, having studied the location with satellite mapping for many months. It's where they'd kidnapped Dexter, a site forever burned into his thoughts.

His stomach rumbled, reminding Danny he was no longer there. He was here in Catalina, where amazing food was just around the corner. The town had three Mexican restaurants serving dishes unlike anything he could find in Colorado. Even so, the green chile stew in Colorado still reigned supreme.

The New Mexicans hated hearing that.

Danny pulled out his phone for a quick search of which restaurants were closest to the La Quinta he'd checked into.

The nearest, Las Chaparritas, didn't open until three o'clock. Sure, he could have driven across town to another restaurant, but Danny was sick of being in the truck. Within a three-block radius were McDonald's, Sonic, and Pizza Hut.

Danny sighed and expanded his search. Six blocks away was a bar and grill called the Dusty Desert, and right across the street from it was Lifted Fire Cannabis Dispensary.

"Jackpot," Danny said, justifying a six-block stroll through town, since there was some green waiting at the end.

He left his belongings in the hotel and marched out the front doors, armed with only his cell phone.

One thing he didn't appreciate about Catalina was how spread out everything was. The blocks appeared bigger than he was used to in Denver, and he soon realized the six-block walk was closer to a mile.

Stretching his legs down the sidewalk still felt good after so much driving. The temperature was warm with a lingering briskness from the cooler morning. The scenery couldn't be more boring, but he appreciated the simplicity of life in the desert. Dirt fields, green and brown weeds, but now and then, a vibrant cactus.

Vehicles passed as he made his way down First Street, the main road through center of town, connecting the north side to the south. If he kept going north beyond the bar and dispensary, he'd run into museums, shops, and government buildings. The police department, post office, courthouse, and city hall all faced each other at the intersection of First Street and High Street.

Danny had to assume the feds would search the compound for Villa. But if they found the place deserted again, they had no justification for keeping resources there to scout the area.

Having nothing but time and money, he'd wait as long as it took. Ages ago, his mother had started saving Armando's death benefits. Instead of living off those funds, she'd kept working and stashed that money in an investment account. All these years later, the account had compounded north of two million dollars.

Tatiana had always said the money was Danny's. She had no need for it. Her hope was for Danny to use it for a life with no worries. She'd raised him frugally enough to probably make that two million last the rest of his life, especially if he could settle down somewhere with a low cost of living.

Getting access to the money would take a bit of work. Danny had no current bank account in his name, but he did have access to his mother's. Nadia had access to the investment account and could move money into Tatiana's checking account for Danny to withdraw with a debit card. There had also been instances where Nadia wired money to Danny in remote locations. He hated sharing access with anyone, even Nadia, but there were times

Danny had to disappear. And someone had to handle matters for his mother.

He never thought much about the money waiting for him in that investment account, opting to pursue a life of purpose and adventure. And when he reached the Dusty Desert, that's exactly what he got.

The bar and grill hummed with a late lunch rush. Mostly retirees sitting at the bar with baskets of french fries, tater tots, and mozzarella sticks. Five tables scattered around the dining area were occupied. The smells of pizza and burgers drifted past, making Danny's stomach churn tighter.

Televisions in each corner showed a variety of channels. Talk shows, highlights, re-runs, even a basketball game in Europe.

Danny moved to the bar and grabbed a stool directly in front of the bartender, a man in his fifties with long graying hair pulled back into a ponytail.

"Good afternoon," the bartender said, slapping the bar top. "What can I get going for you?"

"Is the kitchen open?" Danny asked.

"Always."

"Excellent. I'll have a double cheeseburger with bacon. Fries on the side."

"And to drink?"

"Captain and Coke."

The bartender nodded and turned around to input the food order.

It had long been a habit for Danny to scout the area when entering unfamiliar territory. By the front door stood an old jukebox. A single disco ball hung from the ceiling. Tejano music blared from the kitchen, distorted by the time it reached the dining area.

Danny kept to himself, watching the other men at the bar from the corner of his eyes. The TV above the bar showed a Chicago Cubs game early in the new baseball season. They often played during the day.

Five minutes later, the bartender came out from the back with Danny's food. He placed it on the bar and quickly poured the captain and Coke. "I haven't seen you before. You new to town, or just passing through?"

"Not from Catalina, but have family here." Danny sunk his teeth into the burger, savoring the explosion of juicy beef, bacon, and cheese.

The man eyed him for a moment. "I see. I'll let you eat. Enjoy your lunch."

Danny would normally be a chatterbox with the locals in a small town, but he was too hungry for that right now. He enjoyed a rare moment of peace with his burger and fries.

His drink was more rum than Coke, the perfect way to get an extra tip. Danny washed his lunch down and drew the bartender's attention when the empty glass clanged on the bar.

"Get you another one?" he asked, arching an eyebrow.

"Sure." Danny leaned forward, looking around, then spoke again in a lower voice. "My family told me there used to be cartel activity in this town. Is that still true?"

The bartender took a step back and crossed his arms.

Dammit. I came on too strong.

Danny always struggled with sugarcoating his words. He didn't dig for answers. He asked a simple yes-or-no question and sensed he wouldn't get either of those answers here.

The bartender looked him up and down, surely with questions of his own.

"Who are you?" the man asked, his brown eyes fixed on Danny. The question prompted the other men at the bar to stop their conversation and swivel around on their stools for a look at the newcomer.

Danny shrugged. "I told you I'm visiting family in town. Sorry if I asked something out of line. Wanted to know how safe my family is here."

He grabbed a couple of fries to munch on while the bartender exchanged glances with the other men.

The temperature rose in the room. He'd struck a nerve. Small-town folk loved to gossip, and he'd been hoping to extract info about Los Leones in here.

The man to Danny's left nodded, and this prompted the bartender to speak again. "Sorry about the reaction. We've had both feds and cartel come into this bar. We don't tolerate either of them. Making sure you're not playing for either side."

Danny tossed up his hands and chortled. "The feds are lifeless souls eating off taxpayer dollars. World would be better without them."

This comment earned a round of laughter from everyone at the bar. Danny could adapt to any room of people and speak like them. He considered it his most useful skill in life.

"And I know you're not a cartel guy," the bartender said, pouring Danny's next drink. "You don't look scary enough. No offense."

"None taken."

"This round's on me." He slid the drink over, and Danny took a long swig.

"Thanks. It's just I overheard my family talking about a cartel that used to operate nearby. Apparently their leader broke out of prison. Would hate to see anything happen to innocent people minding their own business."

The bartender planted his hands on the bar and leaned forward, licking his lips. "We don't have any proof, keep in mind. But we talk a lot around here. Have eyes all around town."

Danny pushed his plate back, locking eyes with the bartender. "What are you getting at?"

"Drama is back in our town." He dropped his voice to an octave above a whisper. "And it all reeks of the cartel."

CHAPTER
NINE

DANNY SHIFTED FORWARD on his stool and narrowed his focus on the bartender. "Are you sure about that?"

"Again, I don't have proof. Only suspicion." The bartender shrugged. "I'd say things are more obvious than last time, but we also know what to look out for now. Maybe we're just more aware."

"What *things* are happening?" Danny's heart tried hammering its way out of his chest, so he drew in a deep breath to stay in control.

"You're right about that guy escaping prison," the bartender said. "Victor Villa is his name. That is one dangerous dude."

"You met him?"

The bartender pursed his lips and nodded. "Served him once right where you're sitting. I think it was a test. See, when the cartel was fully functioning in town, I refused to serve them. I didn't want any of their drama in my bar. Some of them would cause a scene—flip a chair or something on their way out, nothing major—while others would simply leave. But I sensed something when Villa came in here. I didn't know who he was, but he had a presence. The energy completely changed inside the bar once he entered."

"He came by himself?"

"Of course not. Had four guys around him. That tipped me off that he wasn't just some schmuck from the cartel. They all catered to him. Funny enough, the guy was nothing but polite and courteous to me. Kept to himself. Left me a fifty-dollar tip after ordering a burger. Naturally, I wanted to kick him and all those men out, but something in my gut told me to shut up and let it play out."

"How did you end up learning who he was?"

"The news, of course. Once he got arrested, word spread across town. Everything got uncovered after that. Lots of those guys had been living in town, keeping a low profile. Never found any sort of central location where they were operating from, but they definitely lived here."

The compound in the desert housed Villa and a select few. Danny knew he made his gang drive out to meet with him a few times each week. They'd pick up drugs and weapons, and leave on their routes across Texas, Arizona, and Colorado.

"If this guy just escaped prison," Danny said, "how could he already have an operation running in here so soon?"

The bartender laughed. "That's like saying the president can't make a decision if he's not physically in the White House. Villa may have been in prison, but he was still calling the shots. Maybe he had a plan in place in case he had to serve time. Definitely had others keeping things running. Sure, we saw the cartel guys less frequently around town, but there were always a few."

"How can you tell someone is part of the cartel?"

"The guys wear a lot of black. That's always a sign, but not a given. Their biggest tell is the tattoos."

"Surely anyone can have tattoos." Danny leaned back, surprised by how much these small town residents had actually gotten correct.

"Not just any tattoo. A lion. Most of them have a lion's face tattooed on their hands. Some had the mark behind their ears, but those seemed rare." The bartender jabbed a finger at the back of

Danny's hand. "Right there. A lion's face no bigger than two inches. It's their gang sign or something."

Los Leones. The Lions.

"And you've seen these guys again? Recently?"

The bartender shook his head. "Not in here. But six months ago, our mayor resigned in the middle of her term. Said she had a family emergency out east and moved away within a week. Like she'd never been here."

Danny's adrenaline increased. "Forgive me, but I don't understand the relevance. You think the cartel forced the mayor out?"

"I'm almost sure of it. The mayor leaving was shocking. She had such big visions for Catalina; it was a devastating blow to see her leave. But when the chief of police retired two months after that, that's when we started wondering if the same thing was happening all over again."

"That happened last time?"

"Sure did." The bartender cracked a grin. "We've been more aware this time around. Chief Rodriguez was born and raised in Catalina. It wasn't his retirement that shocked us—he was approaching seventy and wanted nothing more than to rest. It was his decision to move to Florida that surprised us. That man absolutely hated Florida. Tried blaming the move on his wife, but all their married life, she let him make all the decisions. We don't buy it."

"So your mayor and police chief both left town within the last six months," Danny said, piecing it together. "Who replaced them?"

"The city council president became mayor. Think he's been on the council for three years. No one likes him, which is saying something in this town. He gets to be mayor until we hold an election in November. He appointed the new chief when Rodriguez retired, someone no one was even familiar with. We only have about twenty officers serving Catalina, and he picked one of the newer ones."

"That probably pissed off his peers."

The bartender chuckled. "You know it. Three more resigned on the spot because of it. The new mayor didn't care. Only hired more officers to fill the void."

"You think the cartel was involved with making all this happen?" Danny asked. He'd seen similar scenarios played out across dozens of small towns.

"Hard to say how much they might have influenced it, but it had to be to some degree. I suppose they could have paid the mayor to resign. Even paid off Chief Rodriguez to retire early and move away. After that, I'm not sure what they could have done to make everything else fall into place to favor them."

"That's quite the story." And Danny believed all of it. When a cartel used a small town for their operation, they gradually infiltrated the local government. Assigning a rookie cop to become the chief was an obvious sign. That officer certainly belonged to the cartel and had been planted there for that reason. Now he—in conjunction with the mayor, who had probably been planted by the cartel—had total control over Catalina's police department.

If a resident called in with a concern about dangerous men selling drugs to the high schoolers, that report would die right along with the kids.

"It's a shame," the bartender said, grabbing Danny's empty glass and washing it in the sink. "Catalina is a beautiful town with incredible people. No one here deserves to deal with all this nonsense. We can't exactly call the governor's office and report our suspicions. We fend for ourselves out here. So there you have it. If you see any guys with lion tattoos, just punch them in the face. But don't get shot."

The men around the bar all laughed as the bartender disappeared into the kitchen.

Danny's hope had reached a new high. Los Leones had already been hard at work. They'd known Villa would escape.

Everyone returned to their private conversations, paying no attention to Danny. The main door swung open and two men walked in. They both wore black leather jackets, dark jeans, and sunglasses.

The men sat at the bar, one on each side of Danny. He studied them from the corners of his eyes. The man on his left was bald. The one on the right had slicked black hair, product gleaming under the lights.

The bald man stretched his arm to read his watch, and Danny caught enough of a glimpse to set off all of his internal alarms.

A lion tattoo.

Right on the back of the man's hand.

He looked at the other man. His hand boasted the same figure.

Danny's stomach dropped to his knees. After all that conversation and they just strolled in. He gulped, his palms slick with sweat.

Did they know who he was? Or if he just sat completely still and silent, would they leave him alone?

Danny stared straight ahead at his empty plate, contemplating his next move. He could leave. Toss down a twenty and book it out of the bar. Or he could wait it out and hope for the best.

But hope was for suckers. Danny had eyes on every little movement they made.

The man on the right reached into his pocket and pulled out a switchblade, keeping it beneath the bar.

Danny's vision pulsed, fingertips throbbing with tension. He was out of time.

The only thing within arm's reach was the empty plate. Danny whipped his hands forward to grab it and swung it around to the man's head. He connected perfectly, the plate shattering on impact. Blood spurted from the man's temple as he crashed to the floor, clutching his head.

The men at the end of the bar hollered, but it was all background noise to Danny. He'd saved himself from being stabbed, but the bald man prepared to pounce.

Baldy grunted as he pulled back a beefy fist and powered it into the back of Danny's head. The punch knocked Danny off his stool, but he stayed on his feet. Stars filled his vision as he got his bearings.

The bald man moved surprisingly quick for a heavier guy. He lunged toward Danny, who ducked. Danny took a foot to the face as the big guy flew over him. The blow knocked Danny on his ass, but he spotted a triangular broken chunk of the plate. The sharp point made a better weapon than the other guy's switchblade.

Baldy slid across the floor, now clear of diners. "Cortez!" he shouted, climbing to his feet, death in his eyes.

"I'm sorry." Danny licked blood from a cut on his lip. "Have we met?"

He hadn't recognized the man while side-eyeing him earlier, but he did now.

Freddie Moreno. One of the low-level members of Los Leones. Danny had studied the profiles of all the Leones, as part of their mission to detain them. A mission that never came to fruition.

Moreno reached behind his back and pulled out a revolver. "Don Victor said this message is for you."

Staring down the barrel of that revolver, Danny's life flashed before his eyes. Memories of his youth with his mother. Visiting his father's grave. Nights tangled in the sheets with Nadia.

Facing certain death made all his regrets vanish. He no longer cared about righting his wrongs. Hell, Dexter hadn't even popped into his final thoughts. Go figure.

A gun shot rang out, and Danny braced for that split second before his lights went out.

The top half of Moreno's head exploded into chunks, splattering the walls. A glob of brain matter clung to the screen above him, the European basketball game continuing without a care in the world.

Danny gulped a breath. When he looked to his left, the bartender stood in the kitchen doorway, lowering his double-barrel shotgun.

"I don't know who you are," he said to Danny, "but I'm giving you five seconds to get the hell out of here before I do the same thing to you."

CHAPTER
TEN

DANNY SPRINTED BACK to the hotel, grabbed his belongings, and slid behind the wheel of his truck all within twenty minutes.

It took him nearly ten minutes to catch his breath as he drove south to Las Cruces.

What the hell just happened?

During the drive, he played back the sequence of events, wondering if there was something he could have recognized earlier. Those men had shown up and called him out by his real name, ready to kill him in broad daylight.

Freddie Moreno had looked him square in the eye and tried to kill him.

Danny had a bounty on his head.

I'm going to die here. I need to go back into hiding. Should've never come back.

His heart pounded in his ears, both from the terror he had just endured and the wild dash back to the hotel.

The drive to Las Cruces took him fifteen minutes, since he had to drive slower than normal. The adrenaline flooding his veins made everything move ten times faster. The last thing he needed was to get pulled over by a crooked cop for speeding. Besides, it was hard to fly down the highway while constantly looking in the rearview.

When Danny reached Las Cruces, he drove into the heart of the city, found an Albertson's grocery store, and parked in the thick of cars filling the lot. He let out a long sigh of relief after reaching some semblance of safety. If someone had followed him all the way to this exact parking spot, then so be it. They deserved him.

He remained in the truck, waiting to see if any vehicles pulled up behind him with men jumping out to turn his body into Swiss cheese.

After five minutes, nothing happened. He got out and stumbled on wobbly legs toward the grocery store, reminding himself there was safety in numbers. A public crowd was safer than staying in the car, alone.

Danny hated arriving at a place with no plan. He could be spontaneous when the occasion called for it, but having just dodged death and fled his hotel in Catalina, Albertson's might as well have been a different planet.

He entered the grocery store and took inventory of every visible face. No one paid him any attention as he headed toward the small cafe to his right, pulling out a seat at an empty table.

He ran his fingers along the table, feeling the smooth, cool surface. The scent of coffee filled his nose as he drew in deep breaths, reminding him of his favorite bookstore back in Denver.

A group of college girls giggled after placing their order at the counter, all wearing New Mexico State University sweaters. The Aggies. Danny had become more of a Lobos fan during his months spent watching college sports in Catalina.

College town. Perfect place to hide for a day or two.

Danny had developed a preference for college towns while hiding and traveling across the country. They always had something going on. From boisterous tailgates to intimate poetry readings, he could blend in at these events where cartel gangsters would never think to look.

Plus, all he had to do was shave his face and he could pass for an older college student.

The girls received their drinks and took up a table across the cafe. Danny relaxed with each passing minute. He rose and strolled into the adjacent produce department.

His stomach had been wrung tightly with nerves, so he grabbed a banana and ate it while browsing the store.

I should just go home. It was a mistake coming back to this state. I'll call Nadia, find out where my mom is, and we can move away. I can't take this anymore.

Danny bumped into an employee stocking lettuce under the blasting misters.

"I'm so sorry," Danny said. "Wasn't watching where I'm going."

It was an older man handling the lettuce, his thin white mustache curling up with a grin. "Happens all the time around here, young man. No need to apologize. If we all watched where we were going, wouldn't that take the fun out of life?"

Danny smiled. The old man had a warmth in his voice. "Never thought of it that way, but I suppose you're right."

The man nodded and continued stocking the lettuce.

Danny strolled off in the opposite direction.

The cartel had a handful of elderly members. Lucky ones who had survived their dangerous years. They were often used in advisory roles, preferring to stay out of the day-to-day operations. But a few were always deployed to work undercover and keep an eye out. Stocking shelves at a grocery store was exactly the type of work they would do.

No one suspected a sweet old man to have cartel ties. Danny turned back and looked around the corner. The old man continued tending to the lettuce, placing one at a time while the misters above got his sleeves wet.

You're being paranoid. Exactly why you should go home and forget all about this.

Why were the easiest decisions sometimes the most impossible to make?

Danny left the grocery store in a hurry, compelled to leave all this behind. Dexter hadn't been found. Nothing Danny did now would bring him back.

But he had no intent on getting back on the highway to head north to Colorado. Not after what had just happened in Catalina. He wondered what was happening at the Dusty Desert right now. Dead man on the floor, another unconscious.

What would the man say when he woke up?

Surely the police were there, cleaning up the scene and taking statements from the day-drinking men. Would Danny's name come up?

He didn't see how it wouldn't. Those men were there *because* of him. Neither the bartender nor his friends had any reason to protect Danny, despite the mercy he had shown him after saving his life.

If the police department really was in cahoots with the cartel, then the price on Danny's head had just gone up. They could explain the situation away to the locals. Call it a one-off gunfight between friends having a spat. But the police would know the truth, and word would already be spreading about Danny's appearance in Catalina.

How long until they came down to Las Cruces to look for him?

The police could use their authority to find out where Danny had stayed in Catalina. If the La Quinta had any camera footage of Danny's truck outside their hotel, they'd know which vehicle to look out for, down to the precise license plate.

Danny ran to his truck and sped out of the Albertson's parking lot. He drove toward the college campus until finding a hotel.

Comfort Suites University. Most of the bigger colleges these days had their own hotels the students operated as part of their hospitality programs.

A block away from the hotel was an underground garage, Danny's best chance at keeping his truck out of sight. The cartel was thorough, sure, but they didn't have time to go around and check every underground parking garage.

Needle in a haystack.

Within fifteen minutes of parking, Danny had paid for three nights at the hotel with his mother's credit card, and checked in to his room.

He tossed his backpack on the bed and went straight for the window. His view overlooked the parking lot below and a highway in the distance. A perfect hideout for a few days while things cooled down and he could drive back to Denver.

Danny rummaged through his backpack, its contents spilling out as he searched for his Glock. If anyone came through his door, they'd be met with lead. No questions asked.

The anxiety from the day made him unsure what to do with his time. He needed to do *something*, go somewhere, but his senses forced him to stay put and wait until the coast was clear. He grabbed random objects from the backpack, stuffing some back inside, placing others on the nearby desk.

Beneath the pile of crap lay a matchbook. Seeing it made Danny freeze and sit down on the foot of his bed. He rolled the matchbook from finger to finger. It had to have been buried at the bottom of his backpack for years.

He chuckled and shook his head. "Good one, Dex."

The matchbook had come from a place called Padres Cigars. They had stayed a night in Albuquerque during one of their missions and spent an evening at the cigar lounge. Danny remembered it as the night they'd really gotten to know each other on a personal level. They'd swapped childhood memories, family matters, and talked about all the romantic relationships they had been in.

It was the night they had gone from colleagues to brothers.

Danny squeezed the matchbook and looked out his window at the New Mexico landscape.

"Damn you, Dex. I'm not going home anytime soon, am I?"

CHAPTER
ELEVEN

DANNY SHAVED every last hair off his face, his usually scruffy appearance disappearing with every stroke.

He couldn't remember the last time he had gone with a clean-shaven look, but he had little choice if he planned to hang around southern New Mexico.

Shaving his face was key, making him appear in his mid-twenties. And *feel* sixteen.

Am I getting ready for prom? he thought after his first look in the mirror, patches of shaving cream still needing to be wiped away.

After spending the night with a pistol clutched in his grip—which always led to a rough night of sleep—Danny had gone to the local Wal-Mart to grab items for a better disguise in Catalina.

He had also picked up a New Mexico State hoodie and hat, along with cheap sunglasses. A couple pairs of sweatpants completed his look as a broke college student. All he needed now was a vape pen and a bottle of Xanax.

It was ten o'clock when he put on the idiotic outfit. Backpack slung over his shoulder, Danny had to admit he pulled off the disguise to perfection.

He was ready to return to Catalina.

First, though, he needed a new car. Returning in his truck would only spell trouble. He took one of the electric scooters scattered randomly across the campus, and rode it a half mile west to the nearest Hertz dealership.

Danny pulled out of one of the fake driver's licenses obtained while working undercover with Dexter. It had his actual picture, but the name of Marco Ramirez, complete with an address in Albuquerque.

The best deal they had on a car was a Kia Soul for sixty dollars per day, and he rented it without issue. He looked even more the part of a college student as he pulled off the lot in the all-white compact car.

No one would give him a second glance if they spotted him in Catalina.

He pulled to the side of the street at an empty meter and drummed his fingers on the steering wheel. Part of him still insisted he return home. Even if it was in this ridiculous vehicle. He'd have smooth sailing and could get on with his life.

The only thing waiting for him in Catalina was death and destruction.

After a look in the rearview through his new sunglasses, Danny nodded at himself.

"I came here for one thing," he said to himself, "and that's getting answers about Dex. Nothing else matters."

He admired his disguise, beating himself up for not using one in the first place. If he had, he'd probably be in Catalina making actual progress instead of contemplating life in Las Cruces.

Backing down wasn't something he took lightly, so he put the car into gear and flipped a U-turn to get on I-25 northbound. Doubts bombarded his mind.

What if they had checkpoints right at the Catalina city limits? If the cartel was running the police department, there was no saying what they might do, knowing Danny was on the run. Keeping tabs on everyone coming and going wasn't too difficult to do for a town that had only two entry points. How far would his fake ID take him?

Hi, I'm just coming to Catalina for the weekend. Been a long week at school and I need to blow off some steam.

No college kids went to Catalina to party the weekend away. Las Cruces had much better nightlife. Or they could go the opposite direction to El Paso.

What if he bumped into the man from the bar? Even the bartender might see through the disguise. Would he call the cops on Danny?

He hadn't actually done anything aside from hitting the switch-blade guy with a plate. The bartender had killed Moreno—thank you very much—and let Danny off the hook for any sort of wrongdoing.

Get out of your head.

Since he didn't have to look over his shoulder, Danny arrived at Catalina in ten minutes. No one was waiting for him, and he drove right past the La Quinta where he still had a couple of nights paid for. Danny refused to step foot back in that place. At least not any time soon.

He drove on, needing to see the Dusty Desert. The dispensary came into sight first and he made a mental note to grab some weed before turning in for the night, wherever that might be. He couldn't take another night of tossing and turning, and an indica gummy would surely do the trick.

The traffic light at the intersection turned red just as Danny pulled up. The Dusty Desert had its lights and TVs off. Crime scene tape crisscrossed over the door in a big yellow X.

No cars were parked in front. With the bar to his left, Danny turned right and parked on the sidewalk in front of the dispensary. From his current position, he could see clearly inside the bar, including where he'd sat yesterday.

Those men had entered with complete confidence in what they were doing, even knowing exactly where to sit. Danny narrowed it down to two possibilities. Either he had been spotted during his walk between the hotel and bar, or someone inside the bar recognized him and sent out an alert.

There had been other people in the dining area. Ones he hadn't gotten a clear look at. And none of them were there once the chaos broke out.

They could have tipped off Moreno and fled, knowing what was coming. Danny and the bartender weren't exactly whispering during their discussion about cartel activity in town.

He drove off, refusing to stay in one place too long. Danny planned to take more of a fly-on-the-wall approach for the rest of his time in Catalina. No asking anyone what they thought about cartels. Just sit down, shut up, and listen. There were plenty of other places he could visit on the north side of town. The restaurants up there would be filled with city employees during the lunch hour. Posting up in a corner booth and reading the room wasn't the most thrilling use of his time, but it could pay dividends.

He needed to learn how involved the cartel might be with the local government, including the police force and any judges.

It only took five minutes to reach the other end of Catalina, where there were more businesses and neighborhoods. Main Street bustled with people out shopping and hitting the coffee shops. Downtown Catalina was only four blocks long, but it had art galleries, diners, a library, and several shops ranging from clothing to vinyl record stores.

It had been two years since Danny had last walked Main Street in Catalina. And he'd done it with Dexter.

Not much had changed.

The weather was perfect for an afternoon out. Danny found a parking spot and drew in several deep breaths before stepping out of the little car. He tapped the Glock tucked into the back of his waistband, the hard metal a comfort to him as he walked down the street of the unassuming small town.

Young kids ran and screamed on the playground nearby,

chasing each other and laughing. Danny's heart clenched inside of his chest. He missed how simple life used to be. His mother used to take him to the park every Sunday to play with other kids, and in the summers, they'd stop by a Dairy Queen or McDonald's for a vanilla ice cream cone.

He passed plenty of people as he strolled down the sidewalk toward Main Street. Most were polite and offered smiles. Danny would grin back, but from behind his sunglasses, he was watching everything. Any little movement. People in the distance. If someone didn't smile at him, he'd turn around after they passed to make sure they weren't waiting to shoot him in the back.

Paranoia is a hell of a drug.

The old bookstore he loved was still there, and he planned to grab a new book to hopefully read in the evenings. If his racing mind would allow it.

He started in the bookstore's direction, then paused at the sight of a woman sitting on the curb in front of a hot sauce shop. Her beauty stopped him at first. Long black hair glowing under the sunlight. Skin tanned to perfection.

Danny had only glimpsed her face before she buried it between her hands. Her shoulders were rising and falling.

She's crying.

Concerned, Danny took cautious steps toward her. And he'd be glad he did, considering she would change the trajectory for everything unfolding in Catalina.

CHAPTER
TWELVE

SOFIA HERNANDEZ HADN'T ENJOYED the small pleasures in life since her brother had been kidnapped.

Only three weeks had passed since that regrettable night, and each day brought a fresh wave of worry. Would he still be alive tomorrow? That question rose to the forefront of her thoughts every morning, usually when she robotically brushed her teeth and stared at herself in the mirror, wondering how her little brother had gotten caught up in such a mess.

Idiot.

But she loved him. And had promised her parents she'd look after him. They had retired and moved to Mexico to enjoy their final years on a beachfront property while Sofia and Santiago stayed in their hometown of Catalina. They had their friends, jobs, and every meaningful memory there. Neither had ever considered living anywhere else in the world.

Their parents called Sofia once a week to check on things. She couldn't bring herself to tell them the truth. If they found out, they'd return to Catalina and demand answers. And while that was the correct reaction to such news about their son, their presence in town would only increase the odds of *them* getting caught up in the danger.

Sofia would never be able to live with herself if she lost both her parents and her baby brother.

Getting Santiago back was an uphill battle. When they spoke on the phone, fear always clung to his wavering words. Maybe they held a gun to his head during the calls.

Sofia had just finished her lunch break, having stopped at Sammy's Sammies, a sandwich shop that always had a line out the door during the lunch rush. She had taken four bites of her B.L.T. before calling it quits. That had become the norm over the past three weeks while the secret of her brother's disappearance ate her from the inside.

Santiago had sworn her to secrecy. Their phone calls were random and abrupt, only happening when Santiago could sneak away for a moment. This brought her some comfort, knowing he wasn't tied up in a basement being held hostage.

No, the ropes keeping her brother in place were figurative.

"If I run, they'll kill me," he'd told her. "And then they'll come for you. If you call the police, they will kill me. Then you."

This wasn't mere rhetoric. These men who had Santiago followed through on their word. Every single time.

There had been rumblings of dead bodies found in back alleys. But never any proof. No police reports or news articles. Just words from people who had seen shady dealings and no one to broadcast that message.

Sofia sat on the curb outside of the sandwich shop, head buried in her lap where she stared at the remnants of her lunch wrapped in paper. It was a quiet afternoon in town, only a handful of people wandering around.

A shadow fell over Sofia, prompting her to raise her head. She looked up at a man who appeared to be a college student, but when he spoke, she thought his voice sounded much older.

"Excuse me, miss," he said. "I don't mean to interrupt, but I wanted to make sure you're okay."

Sofia rose to her feet, wiping the back of her pants.

"I'm fine," she replied, sniffling. "Thank you for asking."

"I don't mean to intrude, but you look far from fine."

People in Catalina were caring, but most minded their own business. Sofia didn't know how to feel about this random stranger. He appeared well-intentioned, but she didn't trust just anyone. Especially not now.

"I'm dealing with some family problems," she said. "Have we met before?"

"No. My name is Danny Cortez."

The man stuck out his hand, and she could tell from the weathered look of his skin he was much older than a typical college student. He wore sunglasses, hiding his gaze. Alarm bells rang inside her head and she snapped her hand away from his.

Can't trust anyone.

He whipped off the glasses. His brown eyes lit up once they locked on her, a charming grin touching his lips. You could always tell what you needed to know about a person from their eyes.

Sofia softened, returning the handshake. "Nice to meet you, Danny. My name is Sofia."

"The pleasure is mine. I'm in town for a few days for work—"

Sofia raised her hand to cut him off. "Let me stop you right there. I'm sure you're a nice guy, but I'm not in a headspace to be dealing with dates and men right now."

Danny blinked rapidly, surprised. He was handsome, sure, but Sofia's mind was permanently stuck on her brother. How could she go out and have fun knowing he was fighting for his life every day?

He raised his hands. "I wasn't trying to ask you out. I'm definitely not that kind of guy."

"And what kind of guy are you referring to?"

"The kind who blows through town on a work trip just to hook up with a stranger." Danny shrugged. "All I was going to say was that I'm in town for a few days and don't know anyone. I'd love to have someone who can recommend some places to go, places to avoid. And if you'd like to join me for dinner or drinks, you're more than welcome. The company is paying for everything, so it would be on me. No strings attached."

Sofia looked this man up and down. Living in this small town her entire life, the dating pool was rather limited. She had a firm grasp on Catalina men. Had been hit on by probably all the single ones between the ages of twenty-five and thirty-five. She'd accepted the obligatory date from time to time, just to test the waters. But these Catalina men were all cut from the same cloth.

When she'd spent weekends in Las Cruces or Albuquerque, she'd found the men were different. Less direct and more willing to play mind games. It was a whole different battlefield compared to what she had grown used to.

And this Danny Cortez standing before her seemed a peculiar mixture of both small-town and big-city man.

"Where are you from, Danny?" she asked.

"Denver."

A city bigger than any in New Mexico. Sofia couldn't recall having ever met someone from Denver. They usually blasted right through Catalina on their way to somewhere better.

"Danny from Denver," she said.

He had a presence she couldn't quite pinpoint. He was confident, yet mysterious. Caring, but distant. If she was in any different frame of mind, she'd already be going to lunch with him. Who cared if he was in town for a few days? A girl needed to have fun now and then.

"I get it," Danny said. "You don't want to talk or hang out, and that's totally fine. But I'm someone who enjoys checking out the nightlife in new places. Can you at least tell me if there are any areas I should avoid? Crime-ridden spots?"

Sofia laughed, but hadn't meant to. "I'm sorry, did you say nightlife? You must not know where you are. Restaurants close at eight. The few bars we have usually close at ten—eleven on weekends. And as far as dangerous places…"

Sofia trailed off. No, there weren't bad parts of town. Not in the traditional sense. But Catalina *did* have gang bangers. Not the kind with baggy pants who shot guns out of their car windows. The ones in Catalina were much more terrifying. They moved in silence. Dressed nice.

And they kidnapped my brother.

"I'm sorry?" Danny's voice snapped her back to reality.

No matter what she was talking about, her thoughts always drifted to Santiago.

"There are no bad spots," she said. "Not here."

"That's a relief. People take for granted the ability to walk around town at night. Alone. Not something I'd do in Denver. Glad to know I can do it here."

But you really shouldn't, Sofia thought. *Not if they're out and about. They might take you and force you to work for them. Threaten your life and everyone in it just to bend to their will.*

"Sofia?" Danny said. He had moved his face into her line of vision. "Are you sure you're okay? Was there something else you were going to say?"

Sofia rubbed the back of her head. Had she really spiraled this far out of control? She couldn't even go out in public and have a normal conversation with a random guy on the street? He must think she was going crazy. Or already there.

"I'm sorry." She looked down. The secret had been eating her alive. She hadn't told any friends or family, but her chest was ready to explode. This random man seemed trustworthy enough to at least let her vent. "I'm really distracted. It's my brother. See, he's been taken by the cartel. I think. I don't even have proof of that, but it's my assumption. Unless you know anything about Mexican drug cartels and how I can get my brother, I'm afraid I can't spend any time with you."

Danny took a step back, first looking puzzled by what she had just said. But that confidence swept over his face moments later.

Is he smiling?

He was. But not a smile of delight. It was almost a smirk.

"I think we can help each other out," Danny said.

CHAPTER
THIRTEEN

FIVE MINUTES LATER, Danny and Sofia sat inside a local coffee shop, Enchanted Grounds. Sofia grabbed a table in the corner by the window while Danny ordered them each a cappuccino.

While not a heavy coffee drinker, he couldn't pass the opportunity to sit down with Sofia. He was a staunch believer that people came into your life for a specific reason. Some might call it a coincidence how he'd spotted Sofia crying on the curb. Most would have gone about their day and paid the poor girl no attention. But Danny moved with purpose, turning coincidence into destiny.

He returned to the table with both coffees, admiring the Zia symbol the barista had decorated into the foamy top layer. The café hummed with conversation, drowning out the faint sound of Billie Eilish playing through the speakers.

"Thank you," Sofia said, shooting him a warm smile. "You really didn't need to."

Danny raised a hand as he took his seat. "It's the least I can do."

Sofia drew in a deep breath as she studied her drink. "Forgive me. I'm having a ton of trust issues right now with nearly everyone in my life. How do I know you're not secretly working for the cartel? Maybe you're out here trying to see what people know, report back to them."

Danny leaned back and crossed his arms, lips pursed. If he wanted Sofia's cooperation, he needed to build trust immediately. No more dancing around the truth. "Nothing wrong with feeling that way. I get it. I can't provide you with any physical proof of who I am, but can assure you I used to work for the DEA. In fact, I've been to Catalina before. The last time Los Leones were operating nearby."

"*Used* to be in the DEA?" she asked, her voice raising an octave. "What good does that do any of us? Can you even do anything about this cartel?"

Danny held his gaze on Sofia. Looking away would only make him appear guilty. They could both help each other, and he needed her to see that.

"I'm doing this on my own."

"So you lied?" Sofia stood up, her legs bumping the edge of the table, causing the coffee to slosh over the edge of the mugs. "You said you were here on a work trip and that your company was paying for everything."

Danny nodded, defeated. "Yes, I lied about that. I *am* here for work, if you can call it that. It's definitely not a pleasure trip. There is no company funding this trip. I am. But I have more interest in catching these guys than the DEA does."

Sofia scoffed. "What does that even mean?"

Danny patted the air with his hands. "Please sit back down and I can tell you. I promise, no more lies."

She watched him for a moment, debating her next move. Her gaze burned into his soul, searching for direction. But she sat down, wiped up the spilled coffee with a napkin, and crossed her hands. "Continue."

"Thank you."

Danny told her about Dexter and how everything in his life had gotten turned upside down. Leaving the DEA. Hiding from the cartel and Victor Villa. And, of course, he showed her the chunk of missing ear from the shootout he'd had with the thugs. He closed by stressing the point of needing to find answers for Dexter's family.

Danny took a long sip from his coffee when he finished, glad to have something to coat his throat after speaking for five minutes straight.

Sofia frowned. "I'm convinced. You don't need to say anything more. But if your focus is on Dexter—rightfully so—what does that have to do with helping my brother?"

"I can't just march into their compound and demand answers," Danny said. "I'd be shot dead within five seconds of showing my face. Your brother will need to help me help him. I'm hesitant to watch them from a distance, but I need to learn their patterns and routines first."

Sofia's brows pinched together. "Patterns?"

"Cartels aren't just groups of criminals hanging around all day, waiting for something to do. They're a fully-functioning business. They have employees and daily tasks for those employees to complete. Do you know what they have your brother doing?"

"He's never said, but I don't think it's anything good. I've never heard my brother cry. But he was bawling during our call last week, saying he couldn't believe what he had just done." Sofia shook her head. "I think they made him kill someone. Is that something they do?"

Danny nodded. "I'm afraid so. Your brother is disposable to them. They could have threatened his life if he didn't go out and kill someone. If he's been with them for two weeks and is still alive, then he's playing by their rules. Developing trust with the leaders. That's good."

"It doesn't feel good."

"Of course not. How long was he involved with them before they took him?"

Sofia lowered her brow. "What do you mean? He was never involved with these people."

"You may not want to hear this, but he was." Danny shifted forward in his seat. "The cartel doesn't just kidnap people off the street and force them into working for them. That's too risky and can draw unwanted attention. Santiago probably did something for them. Could have been as simple as delivering an unknown package to a desolate location. Maybe they paid him a couple hundred bucks for the task. But if he kept going back for more of the same, then that's how they sucked him in."

"He wouldn't have done that." Sofia didn't sound too sure of herself. "At least, I don't think so."

"Did he ever leave at random times? Maybe have extra money?"

Sofia sat there with a blank, mortified expression. Her bottom lip trembled as she thought back. "I...I...Yes. He bought me this necklace last month. He'd never done anything like that before."

She touched the silver chain hanging around her neck, a crucifix dangling from it.

Danny bit his bottom lip while Sofia came to this disturbing revelation. She didn't speak again, her gaze wandering aimlessly around the cafe.

"Look," Danny said. "None of that matters right now. What's important is that he's still alive and in contact with you. And I presume he wants to break free from their control."

Sofia jerked her head up and down. "So, how do we get him out?"

"It's not that simple. He needs to stay alive and feed you whatever information he can. I need to know the daily schedule of events at the compound. What time do deliveries arrive? When do they leave? What times of day have the least amount of people at the compound? I really need to know if Victor Villa is there, or has been there. Because if he is, then security around that place is even more complicated."

"But he only talks to me for thirty seconds when he calls," Sofia said. "If that. I can't possibly get all that information that fast."

"Yes, he's probably being watched when he's on the phone. Worried about the cartel overhearing his conversation. It's going to take multiple calls. Next time he calls, don't let him speak. Tell him you have someone helping you get him out, but we need that information. Without it, I can only make a half-assed plan. And that won't cut it against these guys. Not when it's just me taking them on."

Sofia bulged her eyes at him. "You actually plan to do this by yourself? I can't possibly let you. I'm going with."

"The hell you are," Danny said, his tone firm. "I can't describe the level of danger you'd be in. It's reckless for someone with no background in this field to even drive by that compound."

"It's my brother." Sofia's eyes burned with determination. "I have to."

Danny shook his head. "I can get him out myself and get the answers I need. I'd say right now he has a fifty-fifty chance of making it back home. If you enter the picture, that lowers everyone's odds. Do they know about you?"

"Yes," she said. "They've threatened to kill me if he doesn't cooperate."

"And do you have a gun at home?"

"Of course not. Why would I need—"

"Get one. Leave here and buy one. Learn how to use it. You have no idea what your brother is going through. They're going to try and break him mentally. That's how they form loyalty. But not everyone conforms. And if he snaps and disagrees with something they say, you may end up with unwanted visitors. And without a gun, you'll be dead. Or worse. Having that gun will give you a fighting chance."

Tears rolled down her face. "I can't do any of that."

"I'm afraid you don't have a choice, Sofia. I don't say these things to scare you, but to make sure you're prepared for the worst." Danny stretched out and placed his hand on her shoulder. "Just get me that information, okay?"

"And what are you going to do with it?"

"Leave that to me," he said. "I have an idea."

CHAPTER
FOURTEEN

DANNY LET a couple days pass while lying low in Las Cruces.

While there was value to spending more time in Catalina, he had to manage his risk of being exposed. His disguise had worked to perfection the day he'd met Sofia, but no one would believe a college student spending so much time in town, especially while school was in session down the highway. He'd spent those two days shopping for more outfits to fit in with the college crowd. And thinking.

His best thinking occurred in a relaxed state, as rare as that was. The Las Cruces hotel had a recreation room, where he passed the time shooting pool and throwing darts. Not the most thrilling of activities, but it allowed his mind to focus. And wait.

Action movies gave crime fighters a false image. In the movies, the action was constant, one incident leading into another to compact all the thrills into two hours. But the reality was an unbearable amount of time sitting around and waiting for more information. Or paperwork.

In this case, his wait was for Santiago to call Sofia. And even that first call wouldn't yield information, as Sofia would spend their precious thirty seconds explaining what was going on.

Danny understood Santiago's predicament. The poor guy had been forced to do whatever the cartel asked. And until they trusted his loyalty toward them, he'd rarely enjoy a moment of privacy.

They would have taken his cell phone, cutting off his contact with the outside world. Maybe he had gotten a burner phone when he left the compound. Even then, they wouldn't let him leave by himself.

It was possible the cartel agreed to let Santiago check in with his sister. The last thing they needed were search parties snooping around their business. If that was the case, the calls would be monitored by someone standing with a gun pointed at Santiago.

Or if he sneaked off and made a quick private call—which Danny believed was the case—he'd have mere seconds to speak before ending the call. It wasn't worth the risk of being caught.

Maybe I should have Sofia relay the message that the sooner Santiago gains their trust, the more flexibility he'll have to make personal calls.

It wasn't until Danny grabbed new hoodies and hats that an idea steamrolled his thoughts. He could have made progress already had it come sooner. But he didn't beat himself up. A plan was only as reliable as its timing.

Cartels loved recruiting younger men, especially of college age. All Danny had to do was look the part and trust his disguise. And since he'd just shaved off the goatee he'd had for at least a decade, no one would recognize him. He could get work done on his eyebrows to sell his disguise further. Anything to make his face different without permanent changes. Fortunately, the wound on his ear would only be noticed if one was within six inches of his head.

Two years had passed since he'd last encountered anyone from Los Leones—minus the incident at the Dusty Desert. The cartel would have undergone drastic turnover after Villa was thrown in prison. Those who had stuck around were likely promoted. This left fresh blood who wouldn't know Danny Cortez from their own uncles.

If I can get to the compound, I can talk my way into a role with the cartel. Tell them Freddie Moreno suggested I go. They can't confirm with Moreno. I can even play dumb about Moreno's death. Act surprised when they tell me about it.

Danny fell in love with the idea the more he thought about it. And with each passing hour of not hearing from Sofia, he needed to make a plan of his own. Just as he would have had he not met her.

The plan had always been to infiltrate the compound. It was only the *how* he'd needed to figure out.

He grabbed his cell phone and sent a text message to Sofia.

> Please send me a picture of your brother.

Santiago would work the front lines at the compound. Hell, he might greet Danny when he showed up. If Danny knew who he was looking for, it would make matters that much simpler.

Staring over the combinations of outfits he had laid out on his bed, Danny paced the room. All the outfits looked the same. Hoodies. Jeans. Hats. T-shirts. He could grab any pairing and look the part of some hipster college kid.

His cell phone buzzed with a text message alert, and Danny lunged across the room to snap the phone off the foot of the bed.

Anticipating a picture of Santiago, which would allow him to proceed with his plan, he frowned, seeing the text came from an unknown number. He opened it, and the fabric of his world slipped away with each word he read.

> WE KNOW WHAT YOU'RE DOING.

"What the hell?" Danny read the message three more times, his head spinning.

> Who is this?

He waited, the response seeming light-years to come through.

THE DEA.

"The DEA?"

Danny placed his phone back on the bed. He didn't know what to believe. Had he been spotted at the cafe with Sofia? It had been a couple of days. They could have kidnapped her and demanded she share what little she knew about Danny.

She still hadn't responded to Danny's urgent text.

The cartel never cowered away from confrontation if they believed their operation was at risk. They could pose as the DEA, hoping to lure Danny into a trap. And if they used that angle, they certainly knew who he was. And if Villa found out Danny was already snooping around, he was as good as dead. Packing up and leaving town might be his only option. Hell, even crossing the border into Mexico might be safer than sitting in a Las Cruces hotel.

But what if it really was the DEA?

Had Zak put his nose in places it didn't belong? If he faced sharing the truth about what he was researching or losing his job, Danny couldn't blame his friend for throwing him under the bus.

The phone buzzed again.

HELP US GET VILLA.

The cartel wouldn't use their own leader as bait. Danny sat down, his mind working overtime.

If it really was the DEA, how could they possibly know what Danny was up to unless they had spoken with Zak? Only three people had his burner phone number—Nadia, Zak, and now Sofia.

Zak could have been pranking him. It wouldn't be the first time.

Tell me your name

The response came back immediately.

> MY NAME IS NOT YOUR CONCERN.
> GETTING VILLA IS.

Danny let his impulses take the wheel.

> If you're truly the DEA, you can get him yourself.

That ought to show them. Assholes.

> WE KNOW YOU'RE ALREADY THERE.
> ADDITIONAL PRESENCE IN CATALINA
> WILL SET OFF WARNINGS FOR THE
> CARTEL. WE NEED YOU TO COMPLETE
> THIS MISSION.

Danny rolled his eyes. "Up yours."

> I no longer work for the DEA and am not even in Catalina. I'm vacationing in Las Cruces. Get Villa yourselves.

Danny wondered if he might get something from the DEA. He didn't need the money. But if this all went well, maybe a new position with the agency? You gotta shoot your shot, as the kids say.

He'd even be happy if they sent body armor and better weapons. If they actually expected him to take on the cartel and capture Victor Villa, that was the least they could do. Assuming it actually *was* the DEA on the other end.

The more he thought about it, the less convinced he became. The DEA didn't do this. They'd come knocking on his hotel door for a private conversation for Danny's help. There would be an actual plan. No demands. Taking down a cartel boss wasn't some simple task. It required several brilliant minds working in unison on how to best execute such a task.

No response came back. Not from the supposed DEA. Not from Sofia. She was probably at work, so he wasn't too worried. Yet.

Another minute passed, and Danny applauded himself for calling the cartel's bluff. Pretending to be the DEA to suck him into their games.

"Well played, gentlemen," he muttered. "But I'm not new to this world."

He checked his Glock to make sure it was loaded. Just in case someone *did* come knocking at the door.

His phone buzzed. "What now? You've already made a fool of yourself."

But when he read the message, Danny dropped his gun on the bed. This couldn't have been the cartel. And not likely the real DEA, either.

WE KNOW WHERE YOUR MOTHER IS
GOING. TAKE DOWN VILLA AND WE'LL
LET HER LIVE.

IT ALL BEGINS WITH CHAOS, Danny thought.

Any hopes of peaceful days were dashed the second he turned on the TV later that evening. His mind raced. Anxious. Unsure what to do. His mother being endangered was not part of the plan. Well, endangered by the DEA.

Still need to get that damn gummy.

His plans with Nadia would keep his mother off the grid from the cartel. He hadn't known there were others he needed to worry about.

Danny had called Nadia immediately after receiving the last text message. She hadn't answered, so he'd left a message.

Still no response.

He replied to the mysterious DEA contact—which he still didn't believe was the actual DEA—and said he'd complete the job. They moved right past the negotiation phase and made Danny their puppet with fifteen simple words. He refused to let his mom fall victim because of his actions.

They hadn't responded, either.

Whoever was pulling the strings had cranked up the heat. The Channel Nine news station for Las Cruces covered a breaking story.

A balding man in glasses spoke to the camera, the graphic showing his name as David Knox.

"A police officer was shot and killed in Catalina just thirty minutes ago," Knox said. The feed switched to a portrait of a uniformed officer. "Officer Jack Lopez was murdered in a drive-by shooting while walking to his patrol car after his lunch break. Authorities are looking for an all-black car that sped away after the attack."

The coverage changed to an interview with an eyewitness, a man in his forties with shock still smeared across his face. "I thought someone was setting off fireworks. When I looked over, I saw the black car speeding off, and a body on the ground. Didn't even know it was a police officer until a group of us ran over."

Knox returned to the screen from his anchor desk. "The shooting took place right outside of a local sandwich shop, Sammy's Sammies. Las Cruces police will assist the investigation and manhunt. Anyone who spots the vehicle is asked to call the police immediately. Do not approach the car, as the occupant is considered armed and dangerous."

Danny's phone rang. Sofia's number lit up the screen.

He answered after two rings. "Hello?"

"Danny," she said. "Thank God. Have you seen the news?"

"I was just watching. Are you okay?"

"I'm physically fine, but not really doing well." The phone crackled with her breathing. "Can you come meet me? We need to talk."

"Where?"

"Las Chaparritas. It's a restaurant on the north side of town. Far enough away from all this madness. Do you know it?"

Danny drooled at the mere mention of it. "Yes. I can be there in fifteen minutes."

"I'll head there now and get us a table. See you soon."

They hung up, and Danny changed into a college-kid outfit—black hoodie, jeans, and a different ballcap—and tucked the Glock into the back of his waistband. He'd debated ditching the disguise for dinner, but couldn't take any chances while in Catalina. Especially right after a catastrophe.

He went to his rental car, eyes peeled for anything out of the ordinary, and hopped on the highway. Ever since getting those text messages from the DEA, he couldn't shake the feeling he was being watched.

He also kept thinking back to the flowers left at his mother's room. And the note. Who had really left them?

Danny shook his head free of the thoughts when he arrived in Catalina. He bypassed the southern exit from I-25 and took the northern one closer to the restaurant. Cutting through downtown was out of the question.

The restaurant was part of a strip, sandwiched between a dry cleaner's and a tax office. The parking lot was across the street, and he took a spot along the front row facing the restaurant.

He hurried across the road and stepped into Las Chaparritas. Ranchero music played softly through the speakers. Servers hustled across the dining area, carrying trays of sizzling fajitas, jumbo margaritas, and bowls of chips and salsa. Patrons sat around their tables, laughing with their friends and family, munching their food between conversation.

Have you ever seen a depressed person in a Mexican restaurant?

His mother had asked him that once. She had taken him out to eat one night after a rough day in high school. Danny had been dumped by his first love and suffered a knee injury in basketball practice that had wound up ending his season.

Something about that initial chip and salsa hitting his lips changed his mood entirely. Then the tacos. Now that he was an adult, he could add margaritas to the rotation.

He found Sofia seated at a table along the back wall, already halfway through a margarita of her own.

"Didn't realize we're partying tonight," Danny said as he sat down across from her.

"This isn't a celebratory marg," she replied, her eyes heavy and puffy. "I'm just hoping it can settle my nerves."

"That makes two of us." Danny waved the nearest server over and ordered a margarita. "I have some news, but you go first. What did you call me out of my hotel paradise for?"

"Santiago called me last night. Late."

She had zero excitement in her voice and let her eyes fall to the table. Meanwhile, Danny was flipping cartwheels inside. Every phone call Santiago made to his sister was one step closer to his freedom—and to Danny's eventual capture of Villa.

"And?" Danny leaned forward.

Sofia responded in such a low tone, he had to lean across the table to hear her. "I think he did it."

Danny retreated and looked around the restaurant for any wandering eyes. No one paid them attention. "Did...the news?"

Sofia only nodded.

"Why do you think that?"

She licked her lips before taking another drink, eventually meeting Danny's gaze. "I didn't get to say anything last night. He called and told me to listen. Said something bad was going to happen today. And if it went wrong, he'd end up dead. He was crying again. He sounded so...horrified."

Danny reached across the table to caress Sofia's hand. "That doesn't prove anything. He may have known about it. Might have even been involved to some extent—maybe he was the driver. But that doesn't mean he pulled the trigger."

A silent tear rolled down her cheek, and she wiped it away. "What the hell is happening, Danny? A murdered cop?"

Danny pulled his hand back and rubbed his forehead. "These things happen when the cartel is involved. I believe they've already compromised Catalina's police department. If that's the case, any officer who threatens to expose them will find themselves in hot water."

Sofia blinked at him through red-rimmed eyes. "That's disgusting."

"I know. But that's the harsh reality once they're in control. Now, this is all speculation. But, killed while walking to his car? Not even engaged with a potential suspect. That's what tells me it's the cartel."

Sofia shook her head. "I just know my brother did it. I feel it in my bones because of the way he sounded."

"We can't assume that. And even if he did, he likely had a gun pressed into the back of his head to make sure it all played out as planned."

"What happens next?"

Danny sighed, and his margarita arrived. They placed a food order. A taco plate for him. Chile rellenos for Sofia. Never a bad choice.

"If the cartel is running the police department," Danny said, "they'll spend the next few weeks with a phony focus on the investigation. News stories will get released about things that slipped through the cracks. Malfunctioning traffic cameras that should have caught the fleeing car. Delayed response to the initial shooting. All these little things that will kill any hope of finding the murderer."

"So it's all just going to blow over like nothing happened?"

Danny nodded. "That's the plan. They'll throw a big, lavish funeral. Make out Officer Lopez to be a hero. But it'll all be a sham. FBI will show up in town at some point. And the police will share all the files from the investigation. FBI will see there's not much more for them to look into. They might poke around before leaving town. And that'll be it."

Sofia rubbed her entire face. "This is making me sick."

"Then let's stop talking about it. We'll enjoy dinner as best we can and get out of here. Whatever will help you take your mind off things, just the say the word."

And for the next hour, they did enjoy dinner.

Sofia poked around her food at first, but ended up eating the entire meal. Danny had no problems devouring his tacos. He led most of the conversation, telling silly stories from childhood. Pranks he used to do in school. Pranks on his mother.

At one point, he drew a laugh from Sofia. The sweet sound of success. And sure enough, they left the Mexican restaurant with no lingering sadness.

They crossed the street together. Danny offered to walk her to her car before setting off back to Las Cruces.

"Thanks for coming tonight," she said as they stepped foot on the lot.

"It's never a problem," he replied. "Glad I could help brighten up your day, even if just for a moment. Where did you park?"

"Way across the lot. Under that light pole."

Danny chuckled and stopped behind his Kia. "Far enough? This is my car. Maybe I should I just drive you over."

Sofia gave him a playful punch on the arm. "So funny. I was raised to always park under a light when possible. Just in case any creepy men are out there."

"I'm just teasing you. That's actually smart."

They started across the lot toward Sofia's old Buick Verano. Their quick stop at Danny's car probably spared both of their lives.

A thunderous boom rocked the silent night. Shards of glass and metal soared through the air, prompting them to drop to the ground. Danny threw himself over Sofia's body to shield her.

Car alarms blared all around the lot. People ran out of the restaurant, pointing at the raging fire just sixty feet from Danny and Sofia.

"What the hell was that?!" Danny cried, pulling them both up to their feet.

When Sofia looked across the lot, she let out a piercing shriek that would echo in Danny's memories forever.

Her car had been blown to pieces.

CHAPTER
SIXTEEN

"LET'S GO!" Danny yanked Sofia toward his Kia.

The heat from the explosion changed the cool spring evening into a scorching summer night. The bystanders across the street remained, terrified to move even an inch.

Danny forced Sofia into the passenger seat, her eyes glued to her car engulfed in flames, jaw hanging open as she made feeble gasps for breath.

They sped out, rubber burning against asphalt, the smoke from the tires a mere droplet of water compared to the blaze expanding through the parking lot.

Sofia hyperventilated, chest heaving violently, while Danny helped her fasten her seatbelt with his free hand.

"Where are we going?!" she finally asked when they reached the interstate. "Aren't we supposed to stay and talk to the police? That's my car. I can't just act like nothing happened."

"You're gonna have to." Danny floored the accelerator. There wouldn't be any police—crooked or not—worried about speedsters, not with a bomb having just detonated in the quaint town of Catalina. "That's exactly what they want. This was either done to scare you into confessing everything you know to the police. Or they meant to kill you and failed."

"Kill me?" Terror consumed Sofia. She couldn't stop craning her neck to see the smoke plumes still rising into the night sky.

"Yes. I told you. They're trying to break your brother. If he snapped, or disobeyed someone, they won't hold back."

Sofia broke into sobbing hysterics as they flew down I-25 to Las Cruces.

"I need you to take deep breaths," Danny said. "You're alive, and that's all that matters right now. We're both alive."

Danny hadn't taken a moment to process the sequence for himself. He had also been a few steps away from being blown into the sky along with the Buick, but that reality hadn't settled in until now.

"They were watching me," Sofia said after a minute of fighting to control her breathing. "They knew I was in that restaurant and were just waiting to kill me."

"I'm not convinced they wanted to kill you," Danny said, the world whizzing by outside the car. "If they did, that's what they would have done. They shot a cop in broad daylight. The explosion was a message."

"And what is that message?"

"A reminder of who's in charge. To not get involved. Or maybe they found out you've been talking with Santiago."

Danny exited the highway, knowing Sofia wouldn't agree with his decision for her safety.

Sofia looked out the window with wide eyes. "Where are we going?"

"I take it you never got that gun?" Danny asked.

She shook her head. "Not yet."

"Then you need to stay with me. Even if you had the gun, you'd still be staying with me. At least until we figure out what the hell is going on."

"And what about my job? My house? I can't just ignore those things."

"You don't have a choice. Are you really trying to be a hero by showing up at work when your life's in danger? If they knew which car is yours, I'm betting they know where you work and where you live. You need to hide for a couple of days. Let this blow over. We'll see if they make any other moves."

Sofia rested her head against the window, more tears rolling down her cheeks. "I can't believe this is all happening to me. I did nothing to deserve this."

Before he could let any feeling wash over him, Danny's cell phone rang, and he whipped it out of his pocket.

"Yes?" he snapped.

"Excuse you, Danny."

Nadia.

"I'm sorry," he said, his tone still short. "Kind of in the middle of something."

"Well, your mom is checked in to her new facility."

"Did you get my last message? You need to scrap the move and send her somewhere else."

"What? Danny, you can't be serious. I'm not going through all this again after getting her moved. She's already taken a liking to the new place."

"They know where she's staying."

"Who?"

"The DEA." How stupid that sounded once it left his lips. "Well, someone posing as the DEA. I think."

Nadia sighed as Danny pulled into the parking lot at his hotel. "I thought the cartel was after your mom. That's what prompted all this. Now you're telling me the DEA is after her? Is she secretly a drug lord in the retirement home community?"

"This isn't a time for jokes, Nadia. My life's in danger out here. So is yours and my mom's."

"You said mine would never be."

"I don't know who we're dealing with right now," he said. "It's not the cartel. Someone texted me with a threat on my mom's life if I don't get Villa. Change her alias. Move her out of the country. I don't really care what you have to do. I just need you to get it done. It might be best for you to take some time away, too."

"I *am* away, Danny. I found a really remote location for your mom. She's so far off the grid here."

"You didn't take her to Chicago?"

"I wanted to, but figured with Villa out, it was best to hide her somewhere better. She's at a location three hours from the nearest airport. Getting to her is a hassle. I took a week off to make sure she gets settled in."

"Okay, I'll take your word for it."

That was all Danny could do. He didn't know, and wouldn't ask, where his mother was. Not on the slim chance someone was listening to his calls.

"I need to get a new burner," he said. "I'll text you from it once I have it. Don't call me on this number unless there's a major crisis, okay?"

Nadia's lighthearted tone had completely vanished. "Okay, Danny. Everything is good with your mom. Trust me on that. Be safe out there."

"Thanks."

He hung up and killed the engine. Sofia watched him with curious eyes.

"Is your mom okay?"

"Everything's fine. C'mon."

He got out of the car and led them to his hotel room, where his belongings lay scattered all around.

"I like what you've done with the place," Sofia said, forcing a laugh.

Danny turned toward her, frowning in confusion.

Sofia shrugged. "Thought I'd lighten the mood."

Danny had held his breath since the moment they sped out of

Catalina. He released a heavy sigh. "Sorry. My mind's all over the place. Didn't think you'd be in a joking mood right now."

"I'm not. But I do feel slap happy, or something. I'm not sure what this feeling is. Maybe I'm just exhausted."

"I know what you're feeling. It's called relief. You're grateful to be alive. Even though you just survived something horrific, part of you is so happy to be here. I felt the same thing after I escaped that shootout with the cartel. Even with a chunk of my ear missing, I got home that night and couldn't stop laughing. I played music and danced, ordered my favorite meal for dinner. Watched my favorite movies. Everything is different after surviving. No more taking things for granted."

Sofia nodded, looking at the several outfits on the bed. "Going to class tomorrow?"

Danny shook his head. "I'll clean that up. You can have the bed. I'll sleep on the floor."

"That's not really necessary—"

"I insist. Would be wrong any other way."

"Thank you." A grin touched Sofia's lips for a moment. "I'm assuming we're going to attempt to sleep tonight, but what do we do in the morning? We're not actually going to just hide out here, are we?"

Hiding was what Danny did best. Preferring to work from the comfort of computer screens, his first assignments that forced him into field work were spent hiding a safe distance away while Dex handled everything else.

"You should get some sleep," Danny said. "It's gonna take you a few days to feel like yourself again. This kind of thing can keep you up. Nightmares are sure to come, if you're lucky enough to fall asleep in the first place."

"That's already been my life these past couple of weeks," Sofia said. "Honestly, tonight seems more like the natural progression of events with everything that's been going on. I couldn't tell you the last time I had a full night of sleep."

"And that's a problem," Danny said. "They sell sleeping pills down in the lobby. I'll get you some. Is there anything else I can get? Probably a toothbrush. Bottle of water?"

"A toothbrush would be great. I'm not sure if they sell pajamas down there, but something more comfortable to sleep in."

"Okay, give me ten minutes and I'll be back with whatever I can find. I'd lend you my clothes, but they're a bit large for you. Make yourself at home. TV remote is on the nightstand. If anyone knocks, don't answer. I have my room key."

He pivoted toward the door and stopped when Sofia spoke.

"Thanks Danny. I appreciate all of this. Really glad I met you."

Danny smiled. Through the red, puffy eyes and streaked makeup from heavy crying, something about Sofia made her look irresistible. He sensed tension between them, and not in a negative way.

She's vulnerable right now. Hell, we both are. Not the time nor place to act on that.

"Me too, Sofia. Me too."

CHAPTER
SEVENTEEN

DANNY RETURNED to his room eight minutes later to find Sofia already snoring on the bed.

Apparently, she didn't need the sleeping pills, but he placed them on the nightstand along with a water bottle. Just in case she woke up later and needed help dozing off again.

The store didn't have pajamas but carried baggy sweatpants and hoodies. Danny bought the outfit, thinking it was much cozier than the jeans and button-up blouse Sofia had fallen asleep in. He'd also grabbed a toothbrush, toothpaste, and a small deodorant for her.

It had been a couple of years since he'd last purchased such things for a lady. Nadia had him pick up items plenty of times on his way home from work.

He also grabbed a new can of shaving cream, now that he needed to shave every morning to maintain his appearance as a young college student. His Tylenol supply was low, so he bought another bottle. Headaches had plagued him in the evenings. No matter how much he hydrated, he couldn't shake them off.

Stress. Always the damn stress.

His prior job with the DEA had caused him great physical harm.

Between the stress-induced headaches and rashes that had accompanied the more intense portions of his assignments, he'd always assumed he'd die of a heart attack at his desk. Maybe leaving that job was for the better, after all.

Except I'm still doing *the work. And not getting paid a dime.*

Danny laughed at himself, scooting closer to the bed, where Sofia had kicked all of his college outfits to the bottom edge. She lay curled up in a fetal position, looking peaceful.

His instinct was to stroll over, plant a kiss on her forehead, and cover her with a blanket. He skipped the kiss but still covered her up, then cranked up the thermostat to seventy degrees. Sixty-five was his norm, but he remembered most people found that absurdly cold. A byproduct of his mother always being too hot.

Sofia stirred while he hauled the clothes to the closet, but never woke. His background in stealth helped him navigate the room in silence.

After picking up the mess, Danny settled behind his laptop at the desk. He closed the blinds, hoping to kill that sensation of being watched. It only helped a little.

The news would have coverage about the explosion in Catalina. But the hotel TV blared the instant it powered on.

Instead, Danny maneuvered to the Las Cruces news website.

In letters that nearly took up the entire the screen, the headline read: CATALINA CAR EXPLOSION!

Danny scrolled down to see the image of Sofia's Buick swallowed up in smoke and flames. He clicked into the article, curious what facts had made the news.

The reporter described the location of the incident across the street from Las Chaparritas. Firefighters put out the fire, but a bomb squad was sweeping all vehicles parked in the lot and in the nearby neighborhoods.

The chief of police, Ezekiel Montenegro, explained they were trying to get hold of the owners of the tax office next to the restaurant, as they had cameras covering the outside of their business.

"We believe the cameras have coverage of the car that exploded. We could not identify the make or model of the vehicle that was destroyed. Half of the car is missing, and our crews are searching for where those parts may have landed. This was a powerful explosion, and we don't believe it resulted from any malfunctions with the vehicle itself. Our suspicion is that this was an intentional act that used explosives regular citizens wouldn't have access to."

How could you possibly know all that? Danny wondered. He jotted down the chief's name, needing to look more into the man who had taken the reins after the town's prior chief had a sudden change of heart and left.

The article continued by asking anyone who witnessed activity in the lot to contact the police department. And if the owner of the vehicle could claim the car to help with the investigation.

The story was still developing.

Danny shook his head. The cartel was done playing nice. A dead cop followed by an explosion surely meant to distract the public from what was unfolding in their town. Danny wondered why no one was speculating. It could have been the cartel, especially since they'd had a presence in the city before. All this, combined with Villa's recent escape from prison, but not a peep about how it all tied together.

Either the residents of Catalina had their collective heads in the sand, or the local news outlets had also been compromised by the same cartel.

Danny closed the news and opened Google maps to view the satellite imagery of where Los Leones had their compound. It was always tricky to find because of the lack of official roads, but Danny had done it enough times that he could pull up the location after a couple of minutes navigating around the general area.

From the satellite view, the compound was invisible to the common observer. What they later found was the cartel had disguised their location from the satellites, painting the roofs the same shade as the dirt surrounding the property. Only a trained eye could spot the vague outline of the structure. Even the carport adjoining the house blended in, leaving no trace of stray vehicles to appear on the maps.

They never skipped a detail.

Danny had gone out once with a long-range photographer. From five miles away, up on a rock, they'd captured photographs of the compound. And they came out as clearly as if Danny had taken them from outside the gates where armed guards marched back and forth all day.

Barbed wire wrapped around the top of a steel spiked fence. The fence covered roughly one thousand square feet, leaving plenty of opportunity for someone to avoid the guards at the only entrance. Only one dirt road led to the front of the property. One would have to drive off-road for nearly ten miles to approach the compound from the rear. And it was impossible for someone to walk up to it either.

They had cameras covering the other areas around the property. Danny had studied the property during his time with the DEA. It was possible they had since installed more cameras, or moved their locations. Likely, in fact.

Cell phone service was limited, at best, in the middle of the desert. Danny actually found it miraculous Santiago had connected with Sofia. He'd spent plenty of days with Dexter in that area, staring at the red X's on their phones, showing zero signal.

Knowing Villa, he'd probably bought a cell tower and had it built nearby.

The thought of barging into that compound kept creeping into Danny's thoughts. He navigated the map to see if he'd missed anything when he had done this same work for the DEA.

He stared at the map as if it would provide the answers he needed. But none came.

Sofia snored and rolled over. She had fallen into a deep slumber. Surviving trauma could do that.

He closed the map and massaged his temples. Danny would

never make any progress on this case from his computer in a hotel room. Nothing compared to being up close and getting a feel for the scenario. He still had his daring plan of approaching the compound and claiming Freddie Moreno had sent him.

Ready to take his mind off the cartel, Danny opened PokerKing and scouted the lobby for a tournament starting soon. He clicked around for fifteen minutes until finding one he preferred. It was only nine o'clock but after a long, horrendous day, he'd be up late into the night. Without Sofia awake to keep him company, he'd try to make a few dollars.

Even as the tournament began, and he fell into the world of calculating pot odds and playing his position, his mind wandered back to the compound. He could close his eyes and see it. Feel the dusty wind whipping across his face.

It was a dreadful place. The one that had taken his partner and friend. Not to mention his ear. But this time around, it wasn't just him in a mess with the cartel. He had his mother to worry about. Nadia. Sofia and Santiago. The entire town of Catalina. Honest people trying to get by in life. They deserved better than corrupt politicians and police.

Danny had no choice.

I have to infiltrate the compound.

CHAPTER
EIGHTEEN

THE HUM of the laptop woke Danny shortly after eight o'clock. Sunlight clawed through the small gap between the drawn shades.

He'd never formed the makeshift bed on the floor, just passed out at the desk sometime after one in the morning. He'd made a deep run in the tournament, turning his forty-dollar entry into a prize of three hundred seventy-five dollars.

He never played for the money, although it was a nice perk for extra nights dining out. Or perhaps an upgraded room on one of his many stays in various hotels across the country.

After wiping the drool from his mouth, Danny spun around in his seat to see Sofia awake.

She sat upright in bed, her cell phone casting a glow across her face in the dark room.

"Good morning," Danny said. He stood up and stretched his arms, his back cracking in several places. "I take it you slept well?"

Sofia covered her mouth while letting out a yawn. "Something about being away from home helped."

"That probably means you haven't felt safe in your own home."

She scrunched her face while pondering the thought. "I guess I never thought of it that way. That's kind of a sick feeling. Maybe just getting away helped clear my mind." She gestured to the stack of clothes on the nightstand. "You got me pajamas?"

"Not quite pajamas," Danny said. "But the next best thing. I can head into town today and get you anything else you need."

"You're too kind, Danny. That's really not necessary."

"It's the least I can do. You've been jerked away from home. Your car is scattered all across Catalina. And your brother is clinging on for dear life with Los Leones. I don't know how long you'll need to stay here. That will depend on what keeps happening around town. Since they targeted your car, I have to assume they're watching your house. Maybe I can see if we can get adjoining rooms here."

"The floor not up to your standards?" Sofia giggled, relaxing for the first time since they had first met. A good night's sleep could fix plenty of issues. Or at least bring clarity to one's mind.

Danny laughed. "The floor would have been an upgrade. I fell asleep at the desk. And now my neck is paying for it."

"Let's just figure out today first. If we can't get adjoining rooms, I don't mind taking turns for the bed."

"I couldn't—"

"Danny. It's fine. I'm a big girl and can handle sleeping on the floor. I was in college once. Slept in bathtubs, on floors, you name it. One morning I woke up face-down in the front yard."

"I didn't take you for such a party girl."

Sofia playfully rolled her eyes. "That's because I'm *not*. Those stories are from the old me. The version of Sofia who left Catalina for the first time in her life. Stepping out of that bubble set something off. Like I had to cram all the fun I'd ever have into those four years."

"You never thought about moving elsewhere?" Danny asked. "Even Albuquerque?"

Sofia sighed. "I think about it every day. And if I can get my brother back safely, I just might move."

Raiding Villa's compound had slowly become less personal for Danny, and more about helping Sofia.

"I can get into that compound. Don't even have to sneak in, either. They'll welcome me with open arms."

"But can you get out?"

"Excuse me?"

"Getting in is great," Sofia said. "Santiago is in. But he can't get out. Can you?"

Hearing it put so bluntly cast a shadow of doubt over Danny. Still, he replied, "Of course I can get out. I wouldn't go in otherwise."

"And you're confident my brother will trust you? What if he's been brainwashed? He could turn on you."

"I don't think he's brainwashed. Just scared. His involvement with that officer's death was intentional. They use that as leverage. If he runs, they'll turn him in. Even if he did escape, he'd be too scared to approach the police. It's all meant to coerce him to stay. But if I go in there and let him know who I am—that I'm working with *you*—well, he'll do anything to get out, I'd imagine."

Sofia nodded. "I need to call work and tell them I won't be going in today."

"Where do you even work? You've never mentioned."

"In a call center for Southwestern Credit Union," she said. "Chain of banks across the state. It's pretty laid-back work."

"I see. No one will raise any hell if you miss a few days?"

"I doubt it. I'm a top employee. If I didn't have to keep it a secret, I could probably tell them exactly what happened last night, and they'd force me to take a week off. Our busy season just ended, so it's a pretty slow time of year for us. Let me call them, then you can tell me about your plan."

Sofia dialed, and it occurred to Danny he didn't know where *his* phone was. He had to get that new burner today anyway.

He looked around the room, gaze landing on the floor, and

found his phone had fallen, knocked off the desk's edge during his sleep.

He leaned down to scoop it up and discovered a new text message. But there was no text. Only an attachment from a blocked number.

Gooseflesh prickled his skin when the image expanded across his phone's screen.

It can't be.

The image showed Dexter tied to a chair in what could have been a basement. Ropes bound his torso, arms, and legs. Tape wrapped several times around his mouth and head. His face was a tinge of red, eyes bulging from their sockets. But those eyes were open. And alive.

"No," Danny said, placing a hand to his mouth.

His brain and heart were processing two entirely different things. His chest fluttered with hope. Dexter's alive? A chance of reuniting him with his family. But logic rained on the party, insisting it couldn't possibly be true. Why would the cartel have kept his old partner alive all this time?

"Everything okay?" Sofia asked, tossing her cell phone aside. Danny hadn't even heard her speak a word on her call.

"No," he said, his voice gruff and raw with emotion. "It's not."

Danny couldn't look away from his phone. He studied the background. The edges. The detail. Surely this had to be one of those images generated with artificial intelligence. The fingers always gave that away. But Dexter's fingers in the picture looked normal. No distortion or abnormalities.

Danny drew a deep breath to slow his thoughts. Then he typed a message in response.

Who is this?

"Danny?" Sofia climbed out of bed and hurried toward him. "What is it?"

He showed her the picture. "That's my partner, Dex."

She looked between him and the picture, covering her mouth with a hand. "I thought you said he was dead?"

His phone buzzed with another message.

> Hello Danny. You know who we are. We need the girl. Give her to us and we'll give your partner back. Just set her free from wherever you're hiding.

Danny gritted his teeth. Sofia read over his shoulder.

"Me?" she asked. "Am I the girl?"

Danny ignored her and responded to the text.

> Send me a live video of Dexter and you have a deal.

"WHAT?!" Sofia shrieked.

"Calm down," Danny said, rising from his seat and facing both palms out. "I'm just negotiating. You're not going anywhere."

They responded immediately.

> You know where we stay. Bring her to the halfway point and we'll bring your guy. If you're not there by three o'clock, he gets a bullet in the head.

"Danny, what the hell are you doing?" Sofia pleaded. "You're not taking me anywhere."

Danny kept ignoring her. He knew what he was doing. He downloaded the image to his phone and sent it to Zakary, followed by a message.

> If it's safe for you, please help determine if this photo is legit. In a serious time crunch.

"Who the hell is that you just sent it to?" Sofia asked, her mouth still hanging open.

"A friend of mine at the DEA. Only person I trust right now in that department. There's a chance he's been compromised, so we may have to move on our own. You need to get ready for the day."

Sofia retreated toward the bed and sat on the edge. "You must be out of your mind if you think I'm getting in a car with you. Not after what I just read. I'm not some bargaining chip in your quest to save your partner."

Danny ran a hand through his hair. "Please get ready, Sofia."

"No," she said. "You'll have to drag me out of here kicking and screaming."

Danny sighed. "I'm not actually trading you for Dex, so calm down. It's a ninety-minute drive to meet them. We have a lot of decisions to make in the next four hours, the most important of which is to decide if this is real. The cartel rarely bluffs. But bluffing and deceit are two different things."

"*We* have decisions?" Sofia scoffed. "You can go play superhero in the desert if you'd like, but I'll be staying right here."

"I wouldn't advise that, either. They know who you are. That's confirmed now. There will be eyes all over the place. Our best bet is to move around. Preferably every day. We can drive at night. Head down to El Paso. Stay in smaller towns between here and there."

"And what? Keep hiding until you swap me for your partner? I know what you're doing. You're buying time."

"We don't have time," Danny said. "We have until three. I'm talking about a long-term plan aside from whatever happens this afternoon."

He grabbed his gun and a handful of extra rounds, dropping the bullets into his hoodie pocket. "C'mon. We gotta figure things out."

"And what's your big plan, exactly?"

Danny stared her in the eye, trying to convey his confidence and control over the predicament. "I'll tell you when we move. But you need to be the bait."

CHAPTER
NINETEEN

THEY DROVE east into the desert at noon.

"You're not saying much," Sofia said. "Considering I'm putting my life at risk, I'd like to know what you have in mind."

"Your life isn't at risk," Danny replied. "Mine is."

And it was. The cartel had no interest in killing Sofia. But Danny wasn't too sure what their intentions were for him. This could be a ploy to shoot him dead in the desert. It wouldn't be the first time. But Villa didn't take swift action when it was personal.

He was a slow burn aficionado. Capture Danny. Torture him. Make him beg to be murdered. Psychological warfare.

The thoughts churned Danny's stomach as they sped down the unmarked dirt road.

"You want me to believe that if something happens to you, they're just going to let me come back to this car and drive home?" Sofia glared at him from the passenger seat. "I'm not an idiot, Danny. Just level with me. What are we dealing with?"

Danny squeezed the steering wheel. "I don't know. If Dex really is alive, then maybe I've never known what we're dealing with. Cartels don't keep people alive for two years to use as a bargaining chip."

"You think the picture is fake?"

"No idea. All I know is that it *looks* real. Am I not supposed to trust my eyes?"

"'Believe none of what you hear and only half of what you see,'" Sofia said. "My dad loved to tell us that growing up."

"If that's true, then I'd have a coin flip's chance of Dex being alive."

He's not alive. I don't need a coin to tell me that. But there's still no proof...

Sofia pressed her head against the window, staring out at the endless miles of desert that lay ahead. "How much longer?"

Danny checked the clock. They had been driving for a little over an hour. "About twenty more minutes. The halfway point is when this road ends and forks into two different directions."

"Tell me the plan." Sofia was no longer asking.

Danny swore under his breath. "My plan isn't concrete. There are unknown factors until we get there. Mainly, how many people they're sending. They know there are two of us, so they'll probably send three people. Always have the numbers advantage if you can. I'm using you as the bait because I think it's me they really want."

"But they asked for me in that text message."

"Of course," he said. "They're not going to ask me to show up on my own. They just need a reason to have me in their sights. I helped put Villa in prison. I know too much about their operation. It's me that worries them."

"How do I factor into this, then? They already blew up my car. I'm not buying your theory that they're not interested in me."

"You don't pose an actual threat to them. They've had your brother for almost a month now, and you haven't gone to the police. They blew up your car, and you still didn't go to the police. If they have their fingers in the department, they'll leak your name out as the car's owner. That will cause people in your life to pressure you into speaking with the police."

"They can't arrest me," she said. "I didn't do anything."

"It's not about that. Cartels are concerned with the flow of information. We don't know what your brother has revealed to them, intentionally or not. So far, you've passed their test. You're not going to out them. And if I die today, you need to stay true to that. Once you get involved, they'll kill you."

"You can't die today. These assholes don't deserve your life."

Danny chuckled. "I'm afraid they don't see it that way. As for the plan. Assuming there are three people, you're not getting out of the car. You'll need to crawl into the driver's seat. I'll talk while I approach them, and hopefully they won't see you moving around. Stay as low as you can. The other thing we don't know is if Dex will really be there. That will change everything."

Sofia shook her head, disgust apparent on her face with each word Danny spoke. "But if he's not, then we're just handing ourselves over."

"We're not doing that. If Dex is there, stay put. They'll have him in the car and won't show him until you step out. Just follow my lead. We'll fake a swap, but I'll be shooting before you get anywhere near their vehicle."

"And if he's not there?"

Danny smiled. "If they actually pull that stunt, then you're going to run them over. Just floor it and smash them all."

Sofia's jaw dropped. "Run them over? I can't do that."

"We're not dealing with innocent old ladies here, Sofia. These are evil men. And they have your brother. They would do the same thing to you if the roles were reversed." He glanced at the GPS. "We're about five minutes out."

Danny's cell phone buzzed. Zakary responded, almost four hours after his initial message.

Picture is real, but not current. EXIF data says it was taken two years ago at Los Leones compound. Sorry.

"Those assholes," Danny said through gritted teeth. He gripped the wheel harder.

Sofia turned her body to face him. "What is it?"

"The picture is old. From when they captured Dex. So we'll be going with plan B. Run them all over. You'll need to keep your head low because they'll start shooting once you move."

"Shooting?!"

"You'll be fine," Danny said, keeping his voice calm. "It's nearly impossible for these guys to hit a moving target, especially with a car zooming toward them. I'll shoot as many as I can while they're distracted."

Danny slowed the car as they approached a fork in the road. He turned right and caught the gleam of another vehicle about a half mile further up. "Only one car. That's a good sign."

Seeing that fueled his confidence. He wouldn't be outnumbered beyond a ratio he could comfortably handle.

"There can still be five people in a car," Sofia said.

"But all five won't get out. Not if it's just me. If it comes to it, hit whoever you can but make the car your priority. If you can ram into the side and jam the doors, that gives us a significant advantage."

"Danny, I don't know who you think I am, but—"

"We're all capable of rising to the occasion when called upon. If you want your brother back, this is your moment. Keep him in your mind the entire time, and you'll be surprised by what you accomplish today."

The other vehicle was parked near a cactus, off to the side of the dirt road. Danny pulled up and stopped his Kia thirty feet away, facing it straight on.

They came in a black Cadillac sedan, windows and windshield completely blacked out.

Danny unfastened his seat belt. "I'm leaving the car in park. Keep the engine running. Don't wait too long. The longer you see us talking, the greater our chances decline. Act fast and be confident."

Sofia snatched him by the arm. "Danny."

He looked at her hand, cherishing her touch on his skin. Even in this twisted moment. "Yes?"

"Be careful," she said. "Okay?"

Danny opened the car door and winked at her. "And you be dangerous. Okay?"

He stepped out and closed the door. A subtle breeze ruffled his hair, a departure from the usual strong winds.

The front and rear passenger doors on the Cadillac opened in sync. Two men in dark suits stepped out.

"Well, well, well," the first man said, walking toward Danny with his arm's outstretched. "If it isn't Danny Cortez in the flesh."

Danny started toward them, so they couldn't spot Sofia maneuvering around in the car. He didn't recognize the man, who wore a thick mustache and sunglasses.

Danny focused on all his surroundings. The second man cradled an AR-15. Finger off the trigger. He was the muscle in this negotiation. Both engines hummed. Danny had considered the possibility of them trying to run him over. As long as Sofia acted first, they'd have no issues.

"Glad you've heard of me," Danny said, raising his hands to show he was unarmed as far as they could tell. He could have the Glock in his waistband aimed at this man within a half second. "Can't say I'm familiar with you. Then again, you're just one of Villa's little puppies. Such a good boy."

"We've all heard of you," the man said, cracking a grin that revealed two golden teeth. "You can call me Diego. That's all you need to know. Don Victor looks forward to hanging your head on his wall."

"Oooh. I'm not the most beautiful of home decor, but if that's what he wants."

Diego laughed and turned around to his partner. "The boss said this guy had a mouth. Such a funny man."

His partner didn't flinch. Only watched the exchange from behind his sunglasses with a flat expression.

"Let's get this over with," Danny said.

Diego took another step closer, and Danny noted the gray streaks in his hair. He had likely been around when Villa was first captured. Who the hell was he? There were nearly fifty names and faces Danny had studied during those days, so it wasn't a stretch for him to have forgotten some. Diego wasn't ringing any bells.

"Quick to deal," Diego said. "I like it."

"Where's Dexter?"

"I'm sorry, who?" Diego grinned, and Danny ached to wipe the smugness off his face.

"My partner, dumbass. Don't play games with me."

Diego cackled. "Ah yes, of course. First, where's our girl?"

C'mon, Sofia. Make a move already.

"She's in the car. You won't see her until I see Dexter is alive and safe."

Diego nodded and licked his lips. "Very well."

Diego snapped, and the rear passenger door opened again. A body tumbled out, hands tied in back, a black cloth wrapped over the head.

"There you go," Diego said. "Now show us the girl."

That's not Dex. Not even close. C'mon already, Sofia. Make a move, dammit.

"What do you even want with her?"

"That's none of your business."

The man posing as Dexter climbed to his feet, and Danny caught the slightest glimmer from the man's rear. He, too, had a gun in his waistband.

Nice try. Today, Sofia. Before we all get—

The Kia's engine thundered to life as the tires screeched in the dirt. The man with the AR-15 didn't waste a second and showered bullets on Danny's rental car.

Danny took the moment to grab his pistol and fired two shots at the shooter. The second landed and sent him to the ground, the AR-15 clattering down next to him.

The Kia zipped past Danny and connected squarely with Diego. He had nothing to smile about anymore. Sofia jerked the car to the right and hit the front passenger door.

It was all for nothing, as two others had already jumped out of the Cadillac. The man posing as Dexter unfastened the ropes pretending to constrain him and pulled the cloth off of his head. Danny recognized him as Alberto Quezada, one of several men the DEA had been trying to capture ever since Villa's arrest.

"Stay down!" Danny shouted for Sofia, not knowing if she could hear him.

Gunshots echoed all around.

Quezada shot at Danny while the driver of the Cadillac fired rounds into the Kia. The third man, who had been hiding behind the Cadillac, jumped out behind Quezada and focused on Danny.

Danny shot three rounds in Quezada's direction while sprinting toward the Kia for cover. One landed in Quezada's chest. The man dropped his gun and clutched the wound, blood spurting.

"Kill him!" Quezada howled, dropping to a knee and leaning against the Cadillac.

Danny shuffled to the other side of the Kia and looked around the corner. He blasted one shot into the Cadillac driver's head and reloaded with the ammo swimming around his hoodie's pouch. His head rang from the chorus of gunfire, but he only had one man left to kill.

Danny's fingertips pulsed against the cool steel of his pistol.

"Lucha como un hombre!" the last man shouted. He sounded crazed. A true lunatic and probably the cartel's killing machine.

Danny hurried back to the driver's side of the Kia, knowing he had seconds to spare before this madman found Sofia.

The second he looked around the back bumper, three shots fired in immediate succession. Danny fell backward, sliding in the dirt as he clambered to his feet.

The man howled laughter. "Danny Cortez no es nada! Ven acá, pendejo."

He had a semiautomatic rifle. Danny's Glock was no match.

The reverse lights on the Kia illuminated. Danny skidded back to the passenger side, clearing the bumper.

Sofia reversed the Kia. The car's movement prompted a fresh wave of gunfire, but Danny heard desperation in the man's screaming. The Kia backed up enough to expose Danny to the lunatic, but the man paid him no attention.

Danny fired six rounds at the man. Three hit his target. He collapsed to the ground.

Sofia jumped out of the Kia and circled the vehicle to find Danny. Her face glistened with tears and sweat. Her entire body trembled as she threw her arms around Danny, her momentum tackling him to the ground. They both lay there, hearts racing, holding each other, surrounded by death.

"Oh my God, Danny," she cried, squeezing him tight. She buried her face in his chest. "What just happened?!"

"It's over." He stroked a shaky hand over the back of her head. "We're alive."

CHAPTER
TWENTY

DANNY CONTEMPLATED everything in his life while they drove back to Las Cruces.

Sofia had little to say, just stared out the windshield peppered with bullet holes.

She finally spoke twenty minutes into their drive. "Twice in two days I could have been killed. I honestly don't know how I'm still breathing right now."

Danny chalked up survival to destiny. One day, a bullet would surely catch him in the head or chest. But until then, he'd continue living.

"We can't keep at this alone," Danny said. "Dex and I couldn't even handle it. And he basically counted as three people in one. That's how good he was."

Just saying his old partner's name sent fresh, searing pain through his chest. If only he could go back to this morning when he'd thought Dexter might still be alive. Now, he'd never been more convinced of the opposite.

Dexter was dead.

"And who do you propose we ask for help?" Sofia asked, her voice weak. "You said we can't trust the Catalina police. I presume that extends to Las Cruces, too. The DEA is corrupt if they're actually threatening your mother's life. So, are you just wishing for Batman or someone to swoop down from the sky to save the day?"

Danny laughed. He hated Batman. The guy wasn't even a superhero. His only power was money and good looks. Now, if Superman could land in Catalina, that would be a different story. "I'm not talking about any law enforcement. We have to be creative. This might take a while." Danny rubbed his temples. "Let's be intentional with our actions and not rush into decisions. Rushing always leads to mistakes, especially when dealing with a cartel."

"So, strangers off the street? What's in it for them?"

"No strangers. We need people we can trust. Since we're on your home turf, we need people *you* trust. Do you have any friends you'd consider attractive?"

This question caused Sofia to sit up. "Excuse me? You want me to judge my friends by their looks?"

"Simmer down. You don't have to be politically correct with me. Surely you have a group of friends. We need the good-looking ones and the smart ones. No offense to the others."

Sofia scoffed at the suggestion. "My friends are all good people."

"I'm not saying otherwise. But we don't need good people. Attractive and smart will help us." Danny cocked an eyebrow. "Did you ever learn about the women during World War II who seduced the Nazis? They'd approach them in a bar, hit on them, kick up the flirting, and get them drunk. Then, when the Nazis got drunk enough, the women would invite them home. Make them think they were getting lucky. But the women killed them instead."

Sofia let her jaw hang. "You want my friends to seduce cartel men? To kill them? I'm sorry, but none of my friends are killers."

"I'll do the killing. What we really need are these men isolated. Picked off one by one. The fewer there are to guard Villa's compound, the better our chances of breaking Santiago free."

"You can't just go around Catalina killing people in my friends' houses."

"Either I kill them, or they kill us. If you haven't noticed by now, that's exactly how things are playing out. We just killed five of them and left their bodies on the side of the road. It won't be long until word spreads. Someone will know that group of men was meeting with us. You can expect a target on our backs going forward."

"There has to be another way," she said. "I can't recruit my friends into this nightmare."

Danny raised a hand in his defense. "Just an idea right now. I'm open to suggestions. I *need* Villa. I won't stop until I have him or he's dead."

He'd been driving at a steady ninety miles per hour down the dirt roads and kept that pace upon reaching the paved highway that took them into Las Cruces. Desperation spread through him during the drive. There were stretches where he wasn't even paying attention to the road, his thoughts wandering to his mother. Then to Dexter. And Villa.

Knowing all three were now interconnected made his blood boil.

"Danny?" Sofia called out. "Danny, our exit!"

His thoughts had been so noisy, he hadn't realized how far he had driven or how much time had passed. Sofia's words broke him out of his trance, and he swerved a lane over to catch their exit.

Sofia clutched the handlebar above her door and let out a soft shriek. "What the hell, Danny? Are you trying to kill us now, too?"

"Sorry. Mind's all over the place."

"If I need to drive, just say so."

Being back in Las Cruces brought back a certain calm. He'd hated being so far into the desert, where only the cartel prowled the region, hunting for prey.

"We're going back to the hotel, right?" Sofia asked.

"Yes. We'll watch the news and see if anything else has

happened. We might be safe at the hotel. They didn't know where we were staying, and so far, no one has been following us. I know I wanted to bounce around, but I think hiding in one spot might work best. At least for now."

"You've gotten us out of two situations. I'll trust whatever you say."

Normally, such a compliment would have stroked Danny's ego. But he was falling apart. He had no plan. No direction. Whatever came next would be as much of a surprise to him as to anyone watching the nightly news.

Without the backing of the DEA and all their technology, as he'd had the last time he faced this same cartel, he had no chance.

His body ached all over. A nail kept hammering in his head. He needed to get his mom and flee the country once and for all. But he couldn't abandon Sofia and leave her to fend for herself.

Ten minutes later, they pulled into the hotel parking lot. Sofia followed Danny up the stairs to the second-floor room, where he headed straight for the bed to lie down.

Finally ensconced? cocooned? confined to the safety of his hotel room, Danny no longer needed to hold himself together.

Images of Dexter filled his head. Memories from their days working as partners. The disturbing photo they'd sent to his phone this morning. His vivid imagination fed him pictures of what they'd done to him. Based on that two-year-old picture alone, Dexter had gone to hell and back. Beaten and abused. Dragged through the desert like roadkill. Why did such atrocious things happen to honest people?

Then Danny pictured his mother. And Nadia. He imagined the cartel doing the same cruel things to them. If that ever happened, Danny couldn't live with himself. He might as well charge into the compound with guns blazing. Kill as many of those thugs as he could before meeting his inevitable end.

"What's bothering you, Danny?" Sofia asked. She sat next to him at the foot of the bed, prompting him to sit upright.

Danny's chest grew hollow, his limbs trembling. Blood rushed to his face, and his bottom lip trembled. "I can't lose anyone else to these monsters. You could have been killed today."

The dam broke and tears flooded Danny's face. He couldn't recall ever crying in front of someone, aside from his mother. He'd never cried with Nadia, even after all the drama with Dexter.

Emotionally absent, she used to call him.

But he wasn't. Danny simply never cried. He often released his emotions through rage. Or late-night gambling on the internet.

These tears, however, weren't anger. They were fear. Fear of a life without his mother. Yes, she wouldn't be around forever. That much had become plenty clear over the past year. But if she left this world *because* of Danny's mistakes...

"Dex is all my fault." He sobbed, not bothering to wipe his face. Conviction filled every word. "I've lost him. I've put you in danger. And now my mom isn't even safe. We have to bring these guys down. Fast."

Sofia ran a hand along his back. Her touch brought an overwhelming sense of comfort. He turned and buried his face against her shoulder. Having the warmth of another caring soul had long evaded him. The lonely nights had piled up, had taken a toll on his psyche.

Sofia brushed a hand across his face to wipe away the tears.

Danny looked up. Their mouths lay mere inches from each other. Her breathing intensified as she gazed into his eyes. When Sofia licked her lips, Danny had to swallow down the frog forming in his throat.

Is this really happening?

They'd just survived a literal hell on earth scenario.

Danny leaned in closer to confirm what he thought was happening.

Sofia pressed her lips against his then their tongues intertwined.

CHAPTER
TWENTY-ONE

THEY ORDERED room service before getting carried away.

Danny salivated over a steak while Sofia dove into a pasta dish. The dinner arrived on a tray, which they placed on the desk and shared the lone chair. Her leg bounced under the desk. Their arms rubbed together each time they reached forward to scoop up a bite. Danny wanted her.

Their kiss had unlocked a new level of trust. The mood was instantly lighter, despite having dodged death on consecutive days.

Maybe evil doesn't always have to win, he thought. *Even in tragedy, good can rise from the ashes.*

He no longer regarded Sofia as someone needing his help, but as someone who could help him. He'd keep her out of the line of danger, but she had plenty of ways to contribute to her brother's eventual escape from the cartel.

"I'm not going to have my friends sneak around with these guys so you can kill them in their houses," she said, munching on the piece of garlic bread that accompanied her pasta. "I have to draw the line somewhere."

Danny could still taste her lips on his. She had a new glow about her.

"That's fair," he said. "Sometimes I start spit balling ideas and most are no good. Slap a piece of tape on my mouth next time that happens."

She giggled, and the sound sent Danny's heart racing. How he hoped to feel her hot breath intertwined with his again. "I do like your idea of recruiting my friends, though. I know they'd be willing to help, so long as it doesn't involve killing anyone."

Danny nodded. "I have some ideas. But first, we need information from the inside. Have you heard from Santiago at all?"

"Not since that day of the cop shooting. Why?"

"Well, not all the cartel lives at the compound. It fits about ten people comfortably, and Villa prefers his best security on the premises. Everyone else travels in for the day. Most of the others stay in Catalina or Las Cruces because they're the closest towns. The daily commute is insane, but anything to maintain their privacy, I suppose."

"And what does that have to do with Santiago? You think he's being treated well since he gets to stay there?"

"Oh, he's not in the house. New recruits get the shed. They use the shed as a temporary shelter. When Villa wants more of his crew at the compound, they need a place to stay."

"A shed? Like he's some barn animal?"

Danny raised a hand, taking a swig from his glass of wine. Sofia had insisted on ordering a bottle to celebrate their being alive. "It's not as bad as it sounds. The shed has about thirty beds. A kitchen and dining area. Running water. All the necessities." Danny glanced at his plate, wishing he had ordered a dessert. "We need Santiago to tell us who leaves the compound on their own. And when."

Sofia checked her cell phone she had tossed on the bed. "What if I don't hear from him soon? What's the plan then?"

"We'll do it ourselves. It will take longer. I'll have to follow them from where they get on the highway. I don't have access to my old database of these guys, but I remember a few of them. And the ones I don't know, we'll have to do more digging on just to make sure they really are part of the cartel. Can't go eliminating people without knowing for sure."

Sofia stared at the floor. "I have a bad feeling in my gut. Am I going to hear from Santiago again?"

"How long has he gone between calls?"

"The longest has been a week. But that's not the point."

"Remember, he's dealing with matters out of his control. They could have taken his phone away. He could be working with people he knows will turn him in if they found out he was sneaking off and making personal calls."

"Or he could be dead in a ditch."

Danny sighed. "Look, I know it's impossible not to worry about your brother, especially after everything we just went through. But you need to take a deep breath and hold on to hope. That's all you can do. We're not getting him back today. Or tomorrow. But we're taking steps to make it happen."

She shook her head. "I just can't believe he put himself—put *us*—into this mess."

Danny stood up and rubbed Sofia's shoulders. "It's not the time to point fingers. He's in this situation, and that's all that matters. We can get him out. With some help."

"And what do you want my friends to do?" Her eyes twinkled as she looked up at him.

"For now," he said, "we need eyes around town. If they're out and about, have them look for anyone who might be part of the cartel. They'll usually dress well. Flashy jewelry. Drive shiny, black cars. Once we learn where they spend their time—mainly which bars and restaurants—I can follow them. I'm only making moves if I have one of them in complete isolation."

"But how long would that plan even last? Don't you think Villa will see what's happening and react?"

"Of course he will. But I don't think he has a full team around him right now. If he really wanted you earlier, there would have been three cars there to make sure you went back to the compound. And since I only recognized one man, that tells me he's had a serious turnover that probably started when he went to prison. That's natural—it's why we cut off the problem at the head."

"But the cartel is still operating." Sofia grabbed Danny's hands, rubbing her fingers along his palms.

"They're a powerful cartel. Villa prepared for every scenario, including what to do if he ended up in prison. I wouldn't be shocked if his escape was outlined in his plans. All he needed were some loyal soldiers to keep the business afloat, even at a bare minimum, until he got out."

"Well, he's out."

"That's why we need to move fast. It takes time to recruit. He'll be bringing in people across the border from Mexico. He demands loyalty over anything else. As he should. If anyone were to turn him in, that would be the end of his entire operation and back to prison he'd go. The prison would tighten the security around him even more. The guards might even look away if a fight were to break out and Villa was outnumbered by other inmates."

"So it's really his *only* chance." Sofia stretched her arms and yawned while Danny returned to his seat facing her.

"Only chance. Last chance. Call it what you want. Every move he makes will be overly calculated. That will work out for us in the long run. The more you overthink something, the more likely you are to make a mistake. We have to be ready for whatever that mistake might be."

"How are we supposed to move faster than him? He has an entire team supporting him."

"That's why we need eyes. Tomorrow morning, I'm heading to Catalina in my disguise. You need to stay here. If they see you out and about, who knows what they'll do."

Sofia scoffed at the suggestion. "I held my own against those guys in the desert. You can't count me as a liability."

"It's not about your liability—it's for your safety. Obviously, you took care of things this afternoon. But that doesn't equate to future success. Clearly they have some angle with you. If you're out of sight, then hopefully you'll fall out of mind."

"If a disguise is good for you, then it's good enough for me. I can dress up like a college kid, too. Besides, why wouldn't you want me in Catalina? I was born and raised there. I know that town inside and out."

Danny looked into her eyes. She stared back with a fire raging beneath the surface. A look that said, *I dare you to stop me.*

"Okay," he said. "But you're not going without a gun. We'll stop in the morning here in Las Cruces to get one, then we'll head off to Catalina."

"You need a new car, too. Unless you think pulling into town in a Kia Soul with dozens of bullet holes is a good idea."

Danny laughed. "You're right. I'll need to swing by another rental dealer. It's probably going to cost me less to have the car repaired myself instead of paying the rental company to deal with it."

Sofia made a sarcastic smile. "You mean their insurance doesn't cover shootouts with the cartel?" She gave a faux gasp of shock, earning another laugh from Danny.

He enjoyed their time together. Even something as massive as plotting to take down a criminal organization was more manageable with her by his side.

"You're soooo funny," he replied, a mock smile on his lips in return. Tomorrow, we get to work. New car. New gun. And I need to get a new phone. We'll start early, so I suggest you call some of your friends now."

CHAPTER
TWENTY-TWO

THEY GOT AN EARLY START the next morning, waking at seven o'clock.

Danny slept on the floor, conceding the bed to Sofia despite her offer to swap places.

They each showered quickly and dressed in their college attire for the day ahead. After a stop at Enterprise to rent a Toyota Corolla, they swung by a nearby cafe to scarf down breakfast sandwiches. Then Wal-Mart so Danny could buy a new burner phone. Finally, they found the only gun shop that opened at eight o'clock and bought Sofia a SIG Sauer P320 along with a fifteen-round magazine.

"Have you ever shot a gun before?" Danny asked her when they stepped out of the shop.

"Went to a shooting range once with Santiago. Didn't do too well but finished better than I started."

"This is an easy gun for beginners. Point and shoot at close range. Not much to it. Light recoil, comfy grip."

"I didn't know you were such an expert."

Danny shrugged. "I study things. Didn't know a thing about guns until I received a service pistol from the DEA. After that, I studied everything I could. I'm no expert, but I understand what is best for certain scenarios."

"And are *you* equipped to take on the cartel?"

"Of course. Bought myself the same Glock after I had to turn in my service weapon. It's reliable. But depending on what we come across, I may need to get something more powerful. An assault rifle."

Sofia shuddered at the mention of such a weapon.

"Let's go." Danny started the Toyota and took them to the interstate, heading north to Catalina. "Did you get a hold of your friends last night?"

"I texted with a few of them," Sofia said. "Not anyone from work, though. I don't want them knowing I'm back in town."

"Anyone ask about your car on the news?"

"Nope. Don't think anyone recognized it as my car. Kind of hard, I suppose, considering how badly it was damaged."

Nerves settled into Danny's gut. Today had to go well to gain any progress. "Where will you be spending time today?"

"Just drop me downtown," she replied. "I'm meeting with some friends at the library. Figure any cartel people won't be there. Or coworkers."

Danny nodded. "Good call."

"I'm not sure what they'll say, but I'm going to ask them to keep an eye out. Not going to mention you. But do you think I should tell them about Santiago?"

"You kind of have to, or else you'll just seem crazy to them for asking to watch out for the cartel for no reason. Make it personal, and they'll feel more inclined to help. Don't position it as your brother being kidnapped, though. That might cause others to sound the alarm. Tell them he's caught up in a situation with them. They might even see him. But urge them to keep matters a secret. The police can't be trusted right now."

"Got it." Sofia spoke with confidence, reassuring Danny.

Five minutes later, they arrived in Catalina. It had only been a couple of days, but the town had a foreign feel to it. Perhaps because of the tension unfolding with each passing day since Officer Jack Lopez was murdered in cold blood.

They fell silent as they drove into downtown. Sofia's eyes kept wandering toward where her car had exploded. Danny gazed at the La Quinta where he had first stayed before a couple of men tried to kill him at the Dusty Desert bar.

They drove by the Dusty Desert, and Danny was delighted to see the yellow tape removed from the door, although the bar still appeared closed. *A step in the right direction.*

Danny pulled up to a stoplight a block south of Main Street and looked over at Sofia. Even in a baggy hoodie and jeans, she still had an appeal he couldn't resist. He imagined being so lucky to bump into someone as beautiful as her on a college campus. Surely he would have ditched class to follow her around.

But they didn't need to do that. They were adults far removed from college and with a daunting task at hand. She met his gaze and smiled.

"I don't know where the library is," Danny said when the light turned green.

"It's the block behind Main," Sofia replied. "In two lights, take a right. Can't miss it."

He pulled up to the library a minute later. "You have my new number?"

"Yes." Sofia had been setting up Danny's new burner while he drove and handed it over. "I transferred the few numbers you had stored on the old one and removed the sim card from it."

"Perfect. Thanks for doing that."

Sofia laughed. "I feel so alive. Just bought a gun. Took out a sim card. Is this what it feels like, being a badass?"

"I wouldn't know."

Sofia slapped Danny on the arm. "You are *so* bad ass. How could you not think that?"

He grinned at her. "I'm just doing my job, whether or not I'm employed. Stay safe out there and call me right away if there are any developments."

Sofia leaned over the center console and planted a kiss on his lips. "I'll see you later."

She stepped out of the car and left Danny with his racing heart as he watched her stroll into the library.

Once she was out of sight, Danny flipped the car around.

The last time he'd studied the cartel's activity in Catalina, he found a couple of their money-laundering businesses.

The main one was a Mexican restaurant called El Sombrero Taco Shop. It was on the east side of Catalina, in the only area one might consider the "rough" part of town. Danny and Dexter had stayed in the neighborhood once and found it mostly quiet. Some juveniles stirred up problems now and then, but nothing more serious than stealing a candy bar from the corner store.

The houses in the area were older and dilapidated. But the few times Danny had interacted with the residents, he found them polite and happy to keep to themselves.

Many in the neighborhood chose El Sombrero Taco Shop over the downtown restaurants. It was also where the cartel usually spent their time. They sold breakfast burritos as early as five o'clock in the morning, and didn't close their doors until ten at night.

Danny drove straight there, checked his appearance in the mirror, and confirmed his Glock was snug in his waistband before heading inside. The sign above the door featured a black sombrero tipped at an angle over the last O in Sombrero. The stucco building had two large windows that allowed him to see inside.

The place was packed mostly with people ordering their burritos at the counter to go. Booths lined the perimeter of the dining area, and a chalkboard next to the host stand asked Danny to please seat himself.

He strode across the dining room, watching everyone from behind his sunglasses. He made it to the corner booth nearest the window, recognizing no one.

The location was perfect. Danny could see everyone entering and leaving the restaurant, along with any activity taking place outside.

Over the next hour, he enjoyed a small plate of breakfast tacos. He'd normally devour them, but since it was his second meal of the young morning, he forced them down one bite at a time.

His server was an older woman who topped off his water every ten minutes but otherwise left him alone. Danny couldn't be sure if the cartel was still running the restaurant.

Until a man in a suit stepped out from the back. He had a wide grin, dark hair slicked to the side, and six rings on different fingers. His black suit had fine pinstripes leading down to alligator boots.

Jackpot.

Danny didn't recognize the man, but he had no doubt who he worked for.

He watched the man give a quick hug to the manager who was taking payments at the front counter, kissing her on the cheek before marching out of the restaurant.

Danny tossed a twenty on the table, ready to follow him out, then froze when a car—an immaculate black Mercedes—pulled up to the curb. Both passenger-side doors opened.

Danny recognized the man who stepped out immediately. It was the man who had arrived at the Dusty Desert with Freddie Moreno. Same slicked hair, and still a cut on his temple where Danny had struck him with a plate. No one stepped out from the backseat, but Danny observed two silhouettes shifting in their seats. The driver remained behind the wheel.

The man in the suit strode down the walkway from El Sombrero and nestled into the back seat.

Plate guy closed the door and returned to his seat in the front, and the car drove off. Danny raced out of the restaurant and jumped in his car to follow them.

CHAPTER
TWENTY-THREE

DANNY FOLLOWED the thugs to the south side of town, where they parked their car in a neighborhood of ranch-style homes.

The area was familiar to Danny, as he and Dexter had rented a home nearby when they were camped out in Catalina. A family-friendly part of town, trees decorated the sidewalks on the block. An elementary school was two blocks away. A woman walked her dog while Danny sat in his car three houses down from where the Mercedes had parked in the driveway.

He watched the men pile out of the car but was too far away to identify any of them. They filed into the house and closed the door. All curtains were drawn shut.

A fluttering sensation filled Danny's stomach. He'd just found one of their hideouts.

They had never pinpointed the cartel's location in Catalina when he and Dexter worked there. Although, to be fair, their focus had been on the compound in the desert.

Danny pulled out his phone and snapped pictures of the house. He zoomed in, hoping to get a glimpse of anything of significance, but the men had secured the place against wandering eyes.

Still, he had tumbled across a gold mine. Part of him wished to barge in through the front door with his assault rifle and riddle the place with bullets. But he didn't know how many people were inside. He'd need to stake out here for at least the rest of the day to see what kind of activity swarmed the serene house on Adams Street.

His cell phone buzzed with a new text message from an unknown number

> You can't keep switching phones. We'll still find you.

"Are you kidding me?" Danny looked around the neighborhood, paranoid someone was watching him.

His phone buzzed again.

> Still no Villa? What are you waiting for?

He sighed in relief, knowing it was the DEA poser and not Los Leones texting him. He could handle the DEA keeping tabs on him. But if it was the cartel, he'd have to constantly check over his shoulder.

Danny texted back.

> Maybe if I had some help, I could move faster. I'm only one guy taking on an entire cartel.

After a minute without a response, Danny opened the map on his phone and dropped a pin on his current location. Then he studied the area.

They were a minute from the highway, making it easy for them to get in and out of town. He noted the nearest grocery store and gas station. Even the cartel had to fill up and buy toilet paper. If Danny could follow them to these locations, he might get a chance to make some magic happen.

There was only one Catholic church in Catalina, in the same neighborhood. These guys always went to Sunday mass to cleanse their souls of all the evil they'd done. Danny only hoped their God wouldn't show grace when he sent these goons to the pearly gates.

The front door of the house opened, and four men strutted out to the Mercedes. Not one of them was the same as those who'd just arrived. They packed into the car and drove off in the opposite direction.

"Okay," Danny said. "One car. At least nine people in the house. Multiple parts of the operation are housed here."

Every bit of information Danny gained was a piece to fit into the bigger puzzle.

It would take a few days to learn their routines. Did they come and go at the same times each day? Did the same groups leave each time, or did they mix it up? Once he learned that part of the equation, he could then follow them to see where they were spending their time away from the house.

"There have to be other cars," Danny muttered to himself. "No way nine of them are sharing one car."

More of the members would be out and about with the other car. That also meant there had to be more than nine people living in the house.

His phone buzzed.

> We don't have long. Villa will be back to full strength soon. Capture him, or we will proceed with our plans for your mother.

Danny ground his teeth.

> Leave her out of this. She has nothing to do with Villa.

His blood boiled. Their initial threat had already pissed him off, and now they doubled down? He *was* trying to find and capture Villa. At least Nadia had gotten his mother safely moved to a remote location. They were already a step ahead of these DEA posers.

> She has everything to do with you. And we
> need your compliance. We already have
> eyes on her. Moving her to upstate New
> York was a smart move.

"Upstate New York?"

They had to be bluffing. They obviously knew she'd left Aspen. But to call out a new location with such confidence? How could they know, unless they'd been following his mother and Nadia?

He stared at the house, his mind tearing in two. These people had no right to apply such heavy pressure on him to do something he was *already* doing. He wanted Villa for personal reasons. But if he had to leave Villa to the authorities to save his mother's life, then so be it.

A man stepped out of the house and stood on the front porch to smoke a cigarette. Danny used his phone's camera to see him better, zooming in. The image was grainy, but the man had a heavy build and a buzz cut. He looked around between each drag, just an innocent man having a smoke on his front steps.

He puffed on his cigarette for two minutes before retreating.

Danny called Nadia.

The phone rang for twenty seconds before going to voicemail.

"Hey Nadia," he said. "Thank you again for helping with my mom. I owe you big time once this is all over. Maybe I can head out to Chicago and take you out for a night on the town. I know I asked to not know until later, but is my mom in upstate New York? I'm receiving threats and need to know how valid they are. Call me or text me to confirm…Bye."

Those three words had come to his lips again, but he held them back.

She doesn't love me anymore. That ship has sailed, amigo.

Danny opened the digital notepad on his phone and started a

log of events. He noted the time of his arrival at this house, along with when the four men had left. The log would help him catch patterns, and hopefully a full schedule of events.

He texted back to his pen pal.

> My mom isn't in New York. Nice try. Seriously, send me help. Even one person, and this can all be done quick and easy. Going at it alone will take time, but I'm not giving up. MAKE YOURSELF USEFUL INSTEAD OF MAKING EMPTY THREATS!

Danny tossed his phone aside, growing irritated with this exchange. He considered ignoring future texts from the unknown number, wondering if the cartel was trying to pull off reverse psychology to capture him. But they'd texted him within two hours of getting his new phone. Not even a cartel as powerful as Los Leones could pull that off.

But the United States government certainly could.

"If you're really the DEA, you'd have resources to complete this on your own." Danny shook his head, feeling crazy for speaking *to* his phone.

> Your mother is in Tupper Lake, NY. Beautiful facility. Like a resort. We don't appreciate you calling your girlfriend. Capture Villa or they both suffer the consequences.

"Girlfriend?" Danny frowned.

He had *just* called Nadia. Or did they know about Sofia? Neither was his girlfriend, but both were involved.

He couldn't call Sofia to check on her. Any number he dialed would be under tight scrutiny from who he was starting to believe really was the DEA. Or at least a powerful government agency posing as the department.

She will be released once Victor Villa is
captured. No exceptions.

"Who, dammit?!" His phone buzzed again, this time loading a
picture.

Staring back at Danny was a photo of Nadia tied to a chair.

DANNY COULD TASTE death in the air as the sun made its descent.

The second vehicle he had predicted showed up around five o'clock that evening. A black Denali with seven people. They all went into the house and stayed until eight.

Sixteen people in that little house.

Danny couldn't believe how many had crammed themselves in there, but their lack of comfort suggested Victor Villa was definitely calling the shots. If Villa told you to sleep on the floor, you might as well get cozy with the rugs during your stay.

Danny's log contained little information so far. But consistency was the key. Unfortunately, Danny had no interest in coming back tomorrow to see if these thugs followed the same routine. Not as long as the DEA had Nadia and knew where his mother was.

He had texted them back, asking why they thought holding Nadia against her will would help Danny focus. They'd never responded, having gotten the desired result.

Danny weighed the pros and cons of getting an AR-15 and eliminating everyone in the house. But they were all armed, too. All sixteen of them. And cartel guys never hesitated to pull the trigger.

Nadia.

Danny couldn't think straight, knowing they—whoever *they* were—had the one woman he'd ever loved. He called Zakary, hoping to press him for information on the mystery texter. Zak didn't answer, and the frustrations boiled over.

Ten minutes past eight pm, two men strolled out of the house. One was the suited man Danny had seen in the morning at El Sombrero Taco. He wore the same outfit and all the flashy jewelry. He rode shotgun while another man with tight cornrows drove the Mercedes out of the neighborhood.

Brimming with anxious energy, Danny fired up his engine, kept the lights off, and followed the Mercedes. He called Sofia, who answered with unexpected cheer.

"Danny?" The background noise suggested she was at a restaurant or bar. "Thank God! I was wondering when you were going to reach out. After all I did with your phone this morning, I never added your new number into mine."

That explains it.

"Where are you?" Danny asked, his grave tone zapping the energy out of their interaction.

The joy in Sofia's voice fell away. "I'm...out to dinner with my friends. We're almost done. Did you want me to order you something?"

Danny hadn't eaten since his two breakfasts. He had no appetite anyway. "No, thank you. I need to know if you have somewhere I can hide something. Maybe a shed or something similar?"

"What are you needing to hide?"

"I'd rather not say."

"Danny, did something happen today?"

He followed the Mercedes on to the southbound freeway. "A lot has happened today, actually. But right now, I may have the opportunity to get something that needs disappearing. I can't keep it at the hotel. Wouldn't be wise."

"Okay?" Concern filled her voice. "You can use the shed in my backyard." She cleared her throat. "Don't you want to ask what I found today?"

He already knew she'd found nothing nearly as valuable as what he had discovered. She would have led with that. "What did you find?"

"I have a friend who works for the city. In the courthouse." The background noise on her end of the line faded, then came the creaking of a door before it banged shut. "She said the police have been acting strange lately. More secretive. Her office was expecting a report from the police department about my car exploding—don't worry, they still don't know it's my car—but none ever came. Her manager reached out to the police, and they claimed they have no report to file. They're chalking up the explosion as a vehicle malfunction and are no longer pursuing leads."

"What sort of report were they expecting from the police?"

"Normally, the police will make their reports and come up with leads. Then they submit to my friend's office for search and arrest warrants. But nothing for this. Granted, cars exploding aren't an everyday occurrence. She seemed pretty disturbed by the whole thing and is wondering what's going on."

Danny narrowed his eyes on her. "You didn't let anything slip, right?"

"Of course not," Sofia replied. "But because of this speculation, I didn't think it was time to ask for help to look out for the cartel."

"That's fine. I found them. Well, at least a decent-sized group of them living on the south side of town." Danny crossed his hands below his waist. "Can you send me your house address? I still strongly recommend you don't go home. Give me at least a couple days to make sure no one's watching your place."

She was silent for a moment. "I really wish you'd tell me what you're hiding. Just so I know."

"I wish I could too," Danny said. "I'll tell you when this is all done. Nothing you need to concern yourself with."

"Are you going to pick me up tonight?"

"I'm not sure. Kind of on to something big here." The Mercedes headed toward Las Cruces and flashed the turn signal to exit the freeway. Danny exited behind them. "Would you be able to stay with a friend tonight? Tell them you're having a plumbing issue or something and can't stay at your house."

"Okay. When will I see you again? I think we need to discuss our next moves."

"It's still possible tonight. But I'd say tomorrow for sure. I'll call you in the morning."

"Okay. I'll send you my address. Be safe out there, Danny."

They hung up, and Danny was proud of himself for not sharing the threatening messages against his mother and Nadia. Had he brought the matter up, Sofia would have surely spiraled out of control. They'd only known each other a few days, but he had a solid understanding of how she handled conflict.

They cruised through Las Cruces, Danny staying about six car lengths behind the Mercedes. He followed them toward the east side of town, where the college campus and plenty of nightlife awaited: dance clubs, late-night dining, a strip club, and a movie theater.

The Mercedes led the way to a nightclub called The Twisted Olive. It had upscale curb appeal. Valet parking out front, neon lighting around the perimeter, and a line of men and women waiting to get inside.

The cartel guys bypassed all the noise and turned at the next intersection, taking an alley to the back side of the nightclub. Danny followed them up to the alley, where he parked and waited to see how far down they went. About seventy-five feet.

He watched them park, and both men stepped out of the Mercedes, hurrying over to a back door and knocking on it.

Moments later, they disappeared into the club.

Danny turned down the alley and parked behind a dumpster thirty feet away from the Mercedes. He pulled out his Glock, heart racing as he jumped out of his car and positioned himself behind the dumpster for a clear view of the backdoor.

I can take on two by myself.

But he wouldn't kill both men. Just one. The other he needed. For leverage. For information. Whatever he could get.

Five minutes passed, and Danny spent the time focused on his breathing. Breath control was everything when performing a daunting task. Like killing a man. The anticipation was the hardest part.

Doubts swirled in Danny's mind. What if he failed? Or they caught him? What would happen to Nadia and his mother if he ended up in jail for murder tonight?

He shook the thoughts from his head. Self-doubt was most destructive against focus.

An hour passed, but Danny hadn't moved. He needed to make progress tonight. No excuses.

The backdoor swung open, and the sound of laughter filled the alley. When the metal door banged shut, Danny peeked around the corner of the dumpster to see the two men returning to the Mercedes.

He eased from his hiding place and gripped the Glock. Saliva had formed in his throat. He swallowed it back down.

Danny crept toward the men, unseen in the shadows until he was just ten feet behind them. The two men detected him at the same time. Both reached for their weapons.

The man in the flashy suit opened his mouth to say, "Who are—"

Danny pulled the trigger. Landed a slug square on his beefy forehead. He dropped to the ground within seconds.

Danny swung the Glock toward the other man, who had his gun drawn.

"Drop it and you'll live," Danny said calmly.

The man licked his lips, debating. "That you, Cortez?"

"Drop the gun," Danny repeated.

The man nodded and let his pistol clatter to the ground.

"Kick it to me."

The man obliged, and Danny now had an FN Five-seven pistol to add to his collection. He squatted down to pick it up, keeping his Glock on the cartel thug.

"Let's go," Danny said.

"Don Victor has every eye in the cartel looking for you," the man said.

Danny smiled. "Then you all must be blind. I've been sitting outside your house all day. Now, get in my car before I put a bullet between your eyes."

CHAPTER
TWENTY-FIVE

DANNY HAD the man take out a rope from the Mercedes trunk.

These criminals were always equipped to tie someone up and toss them to the bottom of a river. It was tricky to maneuver, but with one hand holding the Glock to the back of the living thug's head, Danny used the other to fasten the rope around the man's torso, tying the knot over his wrists behind his back.

He ordered the man to try to break free, searching for any weaknesses in his knot. There were none, so he took him to Sofia's house, going through a side gate into her backyard where a shed waited.

The shed was mainly used as storage. Bins piled high along the perimeter. Yard tools filled the rest of the space. Danny removed anything with sharp edges. The lawn mower, hedge shears, and saws.

"What's your name?" Danny asked once he led the man into the dark shed. He'd found a flashlight and beamed it across his face.

"Go to hell," the man replied.

Danny responded by balling a fist and punching him in the gut with all his force. The thug doubled over, wheezing air from his lungs.

"Tell me your name," he repeated.

The man coughed after absorbing the blow, his eyes bulging and face turning a deep shade of red. Danny grabbed a metal rake and twirled it in the air. "Tell me your name, and I won't use this on you."

"Ramon," the man replied. "Ramon Murillo."

"Murillo?" Danny said, no longer twirling the rake. "As in—"

"Yes. As in brother of Ricardo Murillo."

Ricardo Murillo had been killed in a shootout with DEA agents three years before Villa's eventual capture. Ricardo had been Villa's right-hand man. Danny had little involvement with the case during the time of that shootout, but he recognized the name from the dozens of reports he'd read on the matter.

"You're one of the monsters who killed my brother," Ramon said, spitting at the ground near Danny's feet.

"Was your brother just walking home from church when our people shot him?" Danny asked. "If I recall, he shot at us first. He was operating a criminal enterprise. Drug trafficking, money laundering, fraud. You name it."

"I thought we get due process in this country. Or is that only for the gringos with money?"

"If he hadn't shot at us, he would have gotten his due process. He pulled the trigger first."

Ramon laughed. A sound Danny hadn't expected in the heat of the moment. "You better hope I don't get out of these ropes. I'm going to tear you apart with my bare hands. Then I'll feed you to the coyotes."

Danny grinned in response. "Do you always get so frisky on the first date?"

Ramon growled and lunged toward Danny, eyes filled with rage. Danny swung the rake, slashing his new friend clean across the face.

Ramon shrieked and fell to the floor.

"Ouch," Danny said, blowing an impressed whistle. "Have a

bad meeting with Wolverine? Sorry about that. But how does that old saying go? Play stupid games, win stupid prizes?"

"Just you wait until I get out of here." Ramon still spoke with conviction through his suffering. Blood seeped from his face in four straight lines, each spaced half an inch apart.

Danny tossed the rake aside and pulled out his Glock. He dropped to a knee. "I think it's cute how you think you're getting out of here. You're on my turf now. No one knows you're here."

"Don Victor will find you. And he'll make you squeal like the pig you are."

Danny pursed his lips and batted his eyes. "Oh, sweetie. None of that is going to happen. Here's what *will* happen. You're going to spend some time in this shed. I haven't decided how long yet. I'll be sleeping inside that house, and if I hear so much as a mouse fart coming from in here, I'll be back. And it's going to be worse than the rake. Scream, and I shoot. Are we clear?"

Ramon looked up and spit toward Danny. He aimed for the face, but the wad landed on Danny's shoulder instead.

"I'll let that slide this time. You and I can help each other. You know what happens at the compound out in the desert. All you have to do is give me names and schedules. I need to know exactly when people are moving in and out of that place. Once you've given me sufficient information, I'll set you free. No strings attached."

Ramon studied Danny's eyes, but not even Danny was sure he could believe his own words. Having one of these thugs in his own private custody had awakened his inner savage, the part of his soul that had loved every damned second of working for the DEA and throwing criminals in prison.

"I'm sure you have no interest in talking right now," Danny said, "so I'll leave you to it."

He stood and dusted his pants off before turning around to close the double doors of the shed. He slid the long shaft of the rake between the door handles, giving a tug to ensure Ramon had no way out.

Danny had no way of getting into Sofia's house. Not legally. And he never intended to, either. Ramon would think he'd be nearby.

Instead, Danny spent the night in his car, parked two houses down from Sofia's property. It took about an hour for his brain to wind down, but when it did, he crashed out from the exhaustion of the entire day.

THE SOUND of sirens far in the distance woke Danny the next morning.

His head was cloudy, mouth dry.

He'd slept so deeply, he'd temporarily forgotten where he was. Danny shot up from his slumped position in the driver's seat and looked around his car. Glock on the passenger seat. His gaze traveled out the windshield. A working class neighborhood. Then he saw Sofia's house. Danny's pulse eased.

Ramon in the shed. His friend with a bullet in the head.

I'm a poet and didn't know it.

Danny chuckled. More sirens blared about two miles away.

He checked his cell phone and found a series of text messages from an unknown number.

"Jesus, did this guy write a book?" Danny said as he opened the messages that appeared to have no end.

> Daniel,
>
> May I call you that?

It was always our destiny to one day meet again. I just didn't expect it to be so soon after my escape from prison.

Speaking of, that is quite the story I'll have to catch you up on. But that is not the purpose of this message.

Today we have a problem. You killed one of my men last night in an alleyway. And I assume you killed his companion or are holding him for leverage. At this point, it doesn't really matter.

You've shaken the hornet's nest, and now you must prepare to be stung. I'm a humble man and will always give credit where it's due. You've done a most excellent job of hiding both yourself and your new lady friend. I'll admit she's cute. But you can do so much better, Daniel. You're a man of the world. Cultured. Determined. Why settle for some townie trash from Catalina, NM?

In my dream world, we can settle our differences, and you'll come work for me. You'd be set for life. And the women I have access to... let's just say they make your Catalina lady friend look like the trash she really is.

I can't be too harsh, of course. Her brother is a loyal soldier and I'm happy to have him on the team.

As you can imagine, it's hard for me to trust anyone right now. That said, I'm extending an exclusive offer to you to meet with me in person. No weapons. No games. Just you and me discussing how we can both step away from this situation that seems to keep bringing us together.

If you choose not to work for me, which I expect you will because of your moral compass, then it's my preference to never see you again. I imagine you feel the same.

The offer stands as long as we're both alive.

Now for the unfortunate part of this message.

No one attacks my men and escapes consequences. That's just the nature of running a cartel. These men dedicate their lives to me, so when one gets hurt or murdered in cold blood, it is my duty to respond with a swift and firm response. Anything less and I lose respect from everyone in my circle.

My preference was to have your lady friend in my custody. That sure would have made things interesting, don't you think?

But you're good at what you do. We can't find her yet, but trust that we will. Again, all credit is due.

So we settled for the next best option, which you will certainly hear about soon, if not already. You left me no choice but to flex my muscle, and now innocent people have to die. If you keep picking off my men —kudos, by the way, for your execution in the desert—I will continue to hit back ten times harder. Each act of violence against my men will result in total chaos for the people of Catalina. I have nothing to lose by watching that city burn to the ground. The escalation of those future events is now in your hands.

Best of luck, and I look forward to hearing back soon.

-V.V.

. . .

"What have you done?" Danny said, firing up his car.

He sped out of the neighborhood, driving toward the sirens. More kept coming. And they had to be coming from Las Cruces now. Catalina's police and fire department were not big enough for the number of sirens trumpeting in the quiet town.

And how the hell did he get the number? The cartel wasn't supposed to have the resources to track a burner phone with such ease.

Unless, of course, they had an insider in the government. Danny had long refused to believe his former colleagues could be corrupted to that extreme. But money could sway a man off course. It was the most powerful weapon that had existed in humanity's brief history.

Three minutes later, Danny approached downtown Catalina and ran into a blockade of vehicles stuck behind a half dozen fire trucks and at least twenty-five police vehicles ranging from Catalina, Las Cruces, and even the New Mexico State Troopers.

A crowd of people gathered in the open park across the Main Street strip, where Danny had first met Sofia. They were all pointing and looking up, but Danny couldn't tell at what. The firetrucks impeded his view.

Danny pulled to the side of the road, parked his car, and dashed across the street to join the others in the park.

His phone rang the moment he reached the park. He skidded to a halt when he saw what everyone's gaze was glued to.

Hanging from the traffic light was the body of a young woman. A noose had been fashioned around her neck. Her abdomen was ripped vertically down the center, guts and intestines dangling like the pull strings of a piñata.

People were screaming. Crying. Vomiting in the grass. Even the first responders had ghastly expressions plastered across their faces. They, too, had never seen anything so gruesome.

Danny's phone rang again, and this time, he answered it. "Hello?"

"Danny!" Sofia shrieked. "THEY KILLED MY BEST FRIEND! THEY HUNG HER FROM A TRAFFIC LIGHT!"

CHAPTER
TWENTY-SEVEN

TEN MINUTES LATER, Danny met Sofia at her house.

She said she needed to grab a few things before leaving town. He had to tell her about the man in her shed, and insisted she wait for him to arrive before going into her home.

The moment he pulled up, Sofia jumped out of a car he'd never seen—one she borrowed from a friend. She marched right up her walkway and entered the house, not even looking back at Danny.

After a quick peek in the backyard to confirm the shed was still closed and undisturbed, Danny followed Sofia inside.

He stepped into a foyer with a shoe and coat rack. To his left was a living room, complete with a sofa and TV. On his right was a dining room that connected to the kitchen in the back. He heard thumps and thuds coming from the hallway that led straight back and followed the sounds to the bedroom, where Sofia frantically stuffed clothes into a suitcase.

"Where are you going?" Danny asked, leaning on the door-frame and crossing his arms.

Sofia never looked up and kept grabbing clothes from the closet and dresser. "I don't know. Just not here. I'm going to hit the road and drive. We'll see where I end up. It's clearly not safe here for me or my friends anymore."

She held her emotions together.

"Look," Danny said. "This will all be over soon."

These words made Sofia stop in her tracks. She slammed a pair of jeans on top of the unorganized pile in her suitcase, and turned to face Danny, eyes red and narrow. "Over soon, huh? And how do you know when it's over? When all your friends and family are dead? I'm not sticking around to watch this situation get any worse than it is. I've already been trying to come to terms with losing my brother. But Ashley…"

Sofia trailed off, her entire face quivering while her eyes filled with tears.

"I'm sorry about your friend," Danny said in his most consoling voice. He yearned to hug Sofia. Comfort her. But the heat of her rage from across the room stopped him from making contact. "Villa had no right to do that."

"No right?!" Sofia shouted. "But he did it, didn't he? My friend is dead, murdered, hung from a traffic light for the whole town to see. How *horrifying* for her family. I can't even imagine. You saw it, didn't you?"

"I did. You made the right decision not to go."

"To hell with decisions," Sofia snapped back. "With everything. All this violence circling my life, decisions seem irrelevant. My life is running on pure luck right now. It's a miracle I'm alive to escape this hell. So that's my decision. I'm leaving Catalina, and don't know if I'll ever come back. If you were smart, you'd do the same thing."

"It's not that simple—"

"Isn't it, though? C'mon, Danny, you've been out here risking your life to find what? Proof your old partner is dead? He's dead, Danny. As dead as Ashley is now. Only a fool would think otherwise."

"Are you mad at me? I'm not the one making these things happen, Sofia. My life has been at risk, too, even before I met you."

"Of course I'm not mad at you. Why would you think that? I'm hurt. Terrified. Sick to my stomach. And yes, I'm plenty enraged. My anger is for my brother. *He* brought all this upon our family and Catalina. I know you're trying to make things better. Trying to right a wrong. But you need to know when to cut your losses, Danny. If you're unaware, right now is that time. I'd invite you to come with me. We could drive away and start a new life somewhere else. But you won't."

Danny drew in a deep breath. Leaving Catalina now made no sense. But what would that mean for the town? And could he actually leave? The DEA had no trouble tracking him down. And they held Nadia hostage. Never mind their vague threats about his mother.

"You're right." He tossed his hands in the air. "I'm not leaving until Villa is either dead or back in prison. That's the only way any of this ends."

Sofia laughed, a sound lacking any semblance of joy. "You're going to die, Danny. How do you not see that? Look what they did to Ashley. They didn't even know her. What do you suppose they will do to someone they actually hate? Someone who's killed their own people?"

"I'm aware of the risks. If I had a choice, I'd have been out of Catalina a long time ago."

"You always have a choice, Danny. The world is a big place. You can hide anywhere."

"If only it were that simple," Danny muttered.

Danny had spent enough of his life hiding in the most remote locations he could find in North America. It was plenty easy to find those spots and start a new life. The tough part was losing his sense of self. Few understood the mental toll of living in isolation, pretending to be someone you're not.

"Well, I've seen enough." Sofia had piled clothes in her suitcase and leaned on top of it to zip it shut. "I have no more hope. I may as well leave the only home I've ever known before it gets blown up. Or before I find my brother's dead body hanging from a tree in the park. I'm glad I never told my parents what was going on. Who knows what would have happened to them by now?"

"I suppose all I can do now is wish you luck."

"Thank you for not trying to stop me." Sofia scooped several personal items from her nightstand drawer and tossed them into her purse. Rosaries, family photos, and an old, tattered Bible.

"I have no reason to stop you," Danny said. "Knowing you're safe will be a huge help going forward."

Sofia scoffed. "Sorry to have been such a burden these past few days."

"You know that's not true. And that's not what I meant."

Sofia pulled the suitcase from her bed and dropped it to the floor, extending the handle, and starting for the door. She brushed past Danny, who still blocked the doorway.

"Will you stay in touch?" he asked before she could reach the front door.

Sofia stopped and turned around to face him. "I don't think so. And with me gone, there's no need for you to contact me. I'd prefer you don't, just in case."

Danny nodded. "Understood. I guess this is goodbye then. I'm sorry I couldn't get your brother out sooner. But I'll still be trying. Hopefully, you two can reunite."

She let go of her suitcase and returned to Danny, grabbing him by the face and kissing him on the cheek. "You're a good man, Danny. I'll never forget you. From the bottom of my heart, I don't see how any of this doesn't end in death for you. I hope I'm wrong."

Her face lingered in front of his for a few seconds, her eyes glassy, and that electricity returned between them. Then Sofia pivoted and strolled out the front door without another word.

Moments later, her car started, and she drove off, leaving Danny alone in her silent house.

He looked around, growing uncomfortable. Danny had no business being here. It wasn't even safe for him. With Villa escalating matters to pure horror, it was only a matter of time before his goons raided the home in their pursuit of Sofia.

She'd really left. He couldn't blame her. He would have, too, had it been in the cards.

Just be safe out there.

Danny walked into the kitchen for a better view of the backyard through the window. The shed still had the metal rake positioned between the door handles. The house was silent enough for him to hear the hairs growing in his ears. Murillo had so far obliged. Or maybe he was sleeping and would soon wake to begin pounding on the doors and shouting for rescue.

Regardless, he was in that shed, and Danny planned to let him cook a little longer. The more desperation filled a man's soul, the more likely he'd cooperate.

Danny pulled out his cell phone, troubled at the prospect of multiple parties knowing the activities happening on his supposed burner phone. He read the message from Villa again, still not having responded.

Danny closed the message and opened a new text for Zakary.

> Text received this morning at 7:17 AM to this number. Can you trace where it came from?

CHAPTER
TWENTY-EIGHT

DANNY DROVE for the next ninety minutes, crossing the state line into El Paso, Texas.

This was how he had to buy another gun, in a different state. Someone flexing as much power as Villa controlled the flow of weapons in and out of the area. Any of his goons might spot him at a gun shop in Las Cruces, and he was glad to have gone undiscovered when he'd taken Sofia to buy her pistol.

The certified dealers were his safest bet, no matter which town he bought his weapons in. Cartels didn't exactly care about following the rules and would sell a fully automatic rifle to a teenager if the price was right. Back alley dealings, where anything flew.

The terror inflicted on Catalina made Danny suspect Villa had a more robust reach than just the local police department. Hanging an innocent woman from a traffic light was a power move. A reminder of who was in control.

And the spectacle of it all proved that Villa wasn't afraid. He certainly wasn't worried about the Catalina police launching an investigation. Beyond that, Las Cruces may have been compromised as well. You don't paint a portrait that bloody if you're worried about being caught.

He knows the feds are after him, so why would he have drawn so much attention?

Danny would chew on this question for the rest of the day. There were plenty of possibilities. The scene could have been a decoy. Maybe Villa was headed to Mexico, where he could breathe easier. He always talked about respect among his peers and subordinates. Perhaps that respect was slipping, and Villa needed to send out a reminder.

Or maybe the feds aren't coming for him, after all.

Danny couldn't help but wonder. Why would the people posing as the DEA refuse to send Danny help? If they really wanted Villa, they'd provide reinforcements. It seemed impossible for the entire agency to be hijacked by the cartel. But if it had been, that would explain why a smaller group was moving behind the scenes. Maybe Danny really was their last hope.

The thought motivated him as he arrived in El Paso. If he was the last man standing between Victor Villa and his return to justice, then Danny had an opportunity to be a hero.

This was no longer about Dexter. The world would be better served with Villa removed from it.

Danny parked outside of a shop called Freedom Weapons. Its logo was an image of a scope's crosshairs with the U.S. flag in the middle. *GUNS. AMMO. ACCESSORIES.* ran along the bottom of the sign.

The store had a mostly glass facade with a tint dark enough that nothing was visible from the outside.

A storm is coming. And sometimes you can only fight fire with more fire.

He got out of the car and trudged into the shop. The place was massive, much bigger than it appeared from the outside. Rifles lined the entire back wall. A glass case ran the same distance, filled to the brim with handguns. Racks stood in the middle of the floor with helmets and other protective gear.

A man stood behind the counter, his hands hooked into his jeans belt loops. He wore a button-up flannel shirt tucked into his pants, and a necktie decorated with bald eagles dangled over his belt buckle. He chewed on a toothpick while watching Danny approach the counter.

"Afternoon," he said with a heavy Texas drawl. "What can I help you with, sir?"

"Good afternoon." Danny scanned the selection behind the man before making eye contact. "I'm looking for a semi-automatic rifle. Preferably an AR-15."

"I got plenty of ARs. If you don't mind me asking, what do you plan to use it for? I can narrow your search that way."

Danny paused, unsure how to answer. He finally responded. "Just for recreation. Long-distance shooting at the range. Many of my friends have ARs. Figured I'd join the party."

The man drummed his fingers on the counter. "There are better rifles for long-distance shooting. The AR is most reliable up to three hundred yards. A seasoned pro can get six hundred yards out of it, though. I guess the question is how long-distance are we talking?"

"Three hundred yards should be just fine. We don't usually shoot farther than that."

The man knocked on the counter before turning around. He ran his finger along the wall of rifles, stopping five feet down the row and pulling one from the rack. He returned and placed it gently in front of Danny.

"This here is the finest AR I have. The Daniel DDM4. Updated handgrip to feel like a pistol. Flash suppressor. Silencer. Gas powered. Basically a notch down from what our boys are using overseas. Runs nineteen hundred dollars."

"I'll take it."

The man nodded and strolled in the opposite direction down the counter. "These take 5.56 ammo."

He pulled out a box and placed it on the counter. One thousand rounds in the box, and Danny hoped that would be enough.

"Okay," Danny said. "I'll take the box. And I need the best scope available for the rifle."

The man crossed his arms and leaned back. "You sure this is for shooting at a range?"

Danny crossed his own arms. "Yes. Why do you ask?"

The man studied him, green eyes looking up and down. "Most rec shooters opt for something less powerful. You come in here wanting the best of the best. Forgive me, son, but you don't have the look of a rec shooter. I can see it in your eyes."

Danny gazed back at the man. *Are arms dealers supposed to double as therapists, too?*

"I'm not sure what you want me to say. I just want to show up my friends. They can be a little cocky. What better way than to have a gun better than any of theirs?"

The man tossed his hands up. "Suit yourself. Not my business. Anything else you need today?"

Danny said he would look around, figuring it wasn't the best time to ask for a bulletproof vest. He found the rack of vests in the middle of the floor and browsed through them. After finding one that fit his thinner frame, Danny perused the other wall with boxes of magazines. He grabbed three more to ensure he could reload quickly if it came to it. His vest also had three slots to store the magazines, so it seemed the perfect match.

After strolling past a display of binoculars, Danny grabbed a pair that touted themselves as the most powerful zoom on the market.

He debated buying a protective helmet but decided that might take it too far. Showing up at the compound with such obvious armor would surely invite immediate fire from the cartel.

Nearly three thousand dollars later—and more curious glances from the gentleman checking him out—Danny left the shop with his new AR-15, scope, three additional magazines, one thousand rounds, a pair of binoculars, and a bulletproof vest.

He put all of it in his trunk and headed back to Las Cruces, where he'd hide in his hotel while devising the perfect plan to infiltrate the compound. He still had Murillo to prod information from too.

At least now he was equipped for whatever came next.

He blasted the radio during his return journey, the local station playing an assortment of Pitbull, Shakira, and Peso Pluma. Danny rarely sang, but he couldn't help himself. Sofia had left and was safe from the cartel's reign of terror. And having ammunition in the trunk that would split a man in half helped fuel his confidence.

He still planned to pick off the cartel one-by-one, if at an accelerated rate.

"If Victor Villa wants it, he's going to get it!" Danny shouted as he looked at himself in the rearview.

The man at the gun shop was right. Danny had a look in his eyes. A look of determination. The focused countenance of a man ready to eliminate evil from the universe. Cartel be damned. Danny would drag Villa out by his lifeless ankles.

Visualize yourself succeeding. See yourself achieving your goals.

This was a method he learned in the DEA from a highly acclaimed psychologist. Success visualization was used by world-class athletes all around the world. Picture yourself making the game-winning shot, or belting the walk-off home run, and it would be more prone to happen. Because in your mind, you've already done it.

So Danny did this. Deep in his thoughts, he walked into the compound, shooting his new rifle at will, dropping every cartel thug in sight. Then he marched into the house and unloaded fifty rounds into Villa. At least.

The visualization carried him for the next few minutes until he received a text message that nearly made him swerve off the road.

Danny pulled over to make sure his eyes weren't deceiving him. But it was real.

The message was from Villa.

It was a picture of Sofia tied up and lying on the ground, unconscious. A second message came through, this one only two words of text.

GOT HER!

DANNY DROVE the rest of the way to Las Cruces at a lethal, reckless speed.

He had texted Zakary to follow up with his last request before hitting the road. No response. After reaching the highway, Danny called his friend and left a voicemail. Zak didn't text or call back.

He called Zak twice more during his frantic drive back, leaving more voicemails with increased urgency.

Once he arrived at the hotel, Danny barged into the room and called Zak again. Another nonanswer had him gritting his teeth. He threw his phone on the bed and started packing up his belongings, shoving items haphazardly into his bag. He didn't plan to leave yet but sensed that decision could come any second. Better to be prepared.

Once everything was packed, Danny sat on the foot of his bed, hyperventilating. The walls of the universe closed around him.

No reinforcements were coming. Not even information from the only man he trusted at the DEA.

How the hell did they capture Sofia?

He'd checked out her house and its surroundings both when he'd arrived and upon leaving. Villa had to have had eyes on the house from a distance, because Danny saw no one in any of the cars parked along Sofia's block.

Danny clenched his fists. *Here we go again. Get close to someone and they're immediately put in danger. Why did I have to walk up to her and introduce myself? Why did any of it have to escalate beyond that chance meeting?*

All the progress Danny had thought he'd made had vanished with one simple message from Villa. He was now scrambling with no clear direction for his next steps.

Danny jumped up from the bed and paced. It was the best way to get his thoughts flowing, aside from taking a steamy shower. He'd studied enough about cartels and their leaders to understand their strategies. Every action had a purpose. Nothing was done by chance or impulse.

He has Sofia for bait. For me and her brother. Santiago won't get out of line if he knows Villa is holding his sister hostage. Maybe he's working with the fake DEA people to get me. They have Nadia. Villa has Sofia. And I'm the monkey in the middle.

Danny understood this subtle game of tug-o-war that was being played with his life. He was trapped. If he left Catalina, there was still no knowing where Nadia was being kept. Or what they might do to his mother. If he stayed, his only option was to get past an entire cartel to capture or kill Victor Villa. A man who was completely ready for Danny's arrival.

At least if I die, everyone in my life will be free.

They'd have no reason to hold Nadia or his mother hostage if he wasn't alive. That thought alone brought him a sliver of peace. What appeared like a fork in the road was really a sharp turn. Danny only had one option. One road to travel. And it led to the compound in the desert.

His cell buzzed from the bed. Danny leapt across the room to see Zakary calling him back. He answered without hesitation.

"Zak? Thank God you got my calls. I've been worried."

"Hey, Dan. Sorry about the delay with everything. It's been... chaotic around here."

"What's going on? I've been getting messages from someone claiming to be with the DEA."

"You must not have seen the news. Mildred got sworn in as the Secretary of DHS. Steele is running the DEA in the interim and is expected to be confirmed by the Senate later this month. Let's just say he's not acting like an interim."

Danny lowered his voice, as if someone had just entered the room to eavesdrop. "Is it safe for you to talk to me?"

"Probably not," Zak said. "But it needs to happen. I probably have a fifty percent chance of getting fired, either way. Steele is out of the office right now, so it's as good a chance as any."

"What's he doing over there?"

Zak sighed. "He's not leading as an Administrator should. He's ruling with a vengeance. Called for a complete audit of all active cases and assignments. Moving more agents around. Yanking intelligence from teams who need it. Claims Victor Villa is the biggest threat facing our country right now."

"Who is he assigning to the Villa case?"

"I wish I knew. He's redacted all files related to Villa. Said he's playing it close to the vest and only trusts a handful of people to work on it with him. He's made it personal and his only priority."

"And you're not one of the trusted ones?" Danny asked. "You've earned your stripes at that office."

Zak chuckled. "Well, that's the thing. He's off for his secret closed-door meetings, and has essentially left me in charge of all the other cases. Gave me a title of 'Special Assistant to the Administrator.' Practically the same duties as the Deputy Administrator, but not the pay or security clearance."

"So you're actually running the department while he's playing around with Villa?"

"That's exactly it," Zak replied, lowering his voice. "I've tried finding things out about the Villa case. In meetings, in passing. And nothing. He just tells me he's working on it and to focus on the other cases. I know everything going on in this department except for the Villa case."

Danny's stomach tightened. The text messages he had received were making more sense.

"Is there anyone you can talk to about all this? I'm sure someone wants to know how Steele is running things."

"Mildred is our best bet. But she's been tied up with confirmation hearings and now transitioning into her new role. She's not as accessible to us. I'm friendly with a couple of senators, but not sure what good that would do."

"It might be worth a shot. But I need help, Zak. That's why I called you so many times today."

Danny filled Zak in about the mysterious text messages he'd been receiving about Nadia, his mother, and his ultimatum to capture Villa. Then the messages from Villa himself. And more recently, the murder in Catalina and kidnapping of Sofia.

"Christ," Zak said. "I haven't heard a peep. I saw your message about tracking that phone number. I'll make it a top priority."

"Thanks," Danny said. "Has Steele indicated what happens once Villa is captured?"

"Of course not. All I know is the rest of us are ready for the Villa case to be closed. Things can't possibly get any worse once he's locked back up."

"Or dead."

Zak chuckled. "I'll take whatever I can get at this point."

"Me too. I know where Villa is. Right where he left off at his compound. You can feed this information to Steele. I can't keep going at this by myself. It's getting more dangerous with each passing day."

"I'll try, but don't get your hopes up, Dan. The moment anyone else brings up Villa, he redirects the conversation. Don't you think I've tried sharing notes from your old case? You and Dex damn near had an encyclopedia on his cartel. The moment I mentioned those notes, he redacted them. He doesn't want anyone else having knowledge on the matter aside from him and his select team."

Danny stared out his window. Cars zoomed by on the highway in the distance. Food trucks lined the block below. He couldn't believe everything that had happened today with the end nowhere in sight. "I smell a conspiracy, Zak. You need to find out who Steele is trusting to work on the Villa case. That might shed some light on what's really going on. If he has a confirmation hearing coming up, try to see which senators he's schmoozing with the most."

"You think this is going all the way up to the senate? I don't know, Dan. That's a stretch. Steele is just a little bully kid who the teacher put in charge of the class."

"Like Jack in *Lord of the Flies*."

"Precisely," Zak replied. "I'm not denying there's something personal about the Villa case for Steele. That much goes without saying. But a conspiracy? I don't buy it."

Zak always was an optimist. Refused to see the worst in people, which wasn't an ideal trait for someone working in the federal government.

Steele's takeover sounded hostile and intentional. No Administrator, regardless of which president nominated them, came into the DEA and pulled agents off cases in the middle of their assignments —an unwritten rule.

The point of chaos is to distract from the truth.

Steele was hiding something. And the more drastic his actions, the bigger Danny believed his secret to be.

"He's back," Zak said. "I gotta go. I'll text you back about those messages."

He hung up without another word.

Danny's gut sank a little more. Zak was operating in fear. His friend was smart enough to not get fired over something petty.

But if he did, then Danny really would be on his own.

CHAPTER
THIRTY

THE NEXT MORNING, Danny received a text message from Zak with coordinates.

He was glad the information hadn't come through too soon after their phone call. Danny couldn't handle any more excitement for the day and had been relieved to have a somewhat quiet evening alone at the hotel, once his nerves had settled down.

He'd passed the time getting familiar with his new AR-15. He'd shot ARs a few times at the range, but had never owned one. His protective vest also fit to perfection. Danny practiced how quickly he could swap out the magazines on his new toy, getting his time down to just under two seconds. Shaving another second off that time could be the difference between life and death, so he practiced several times throughout the evening to perfect his motion.

Then Danny had taken a sleeping pill from the stash he'd bought for Sofia. His mind had been too full to relax and drift into slumber on his own. When he'd woken up, his head fog was cleared for the first time since arriving in Catalina. Today, he could finally focus.

He checked his phone to see the message and entered the coordinates Zak sent in the maps app on his burner, leading to the phone's location in the middle of the desert. No surprise there. However, the location wasn't the compound as he'd expected.

It was about three miles northwest of the compound. Even zooming in on the satellite imagery of the area, Danny found nothing. Maybe there was another building meant to blend in with the surrounding desert.

The added mystery piled on additional stress. He'd planned to approach the compound. But with a different location, matters weren't so clear. Was it another compound? A smaller structure? How many cartel members would be there?

None of it mattered now. Danny had to wing it and go see for himself. He wrapped up the AR in a spare jacket and carried it to his car. He had yet to be spotted with it and vowed to keep it that way as long as possible.

Danny got behind the wheel and drove in silence to his destination. No music. No distractions. The ninety-minute drive east of Las Cruces flew by the time he reached a good stopping point.

A mile out from what the map deemed his destination, Danny pulled off the road and kept going until the dirt path was no longer in sight. The land was flat as far as he could see. When he pulled out his binoculars, he wasn't expecting to see anything from a mile out, but quickly discovered a large tent.

It looked roughly the size of a house no bigger than Sofia's. Only it wasn't a house. Tables filled the space covered by a canopy. Five people sat in chairs behind the tables scattered across the area.

"What are you guys doing?" Objects covered the tables, but Danny couldn't make out what they were. Hundreds of cell phones? Why would the cartel have cell phones in the middle of nowhere?

Danny returned to his car and drove another half mile toward the pin on his map. He went through the same routine of going off road by a quarter mile to ensure he wasn't seen. With a better view, all the objects littered across the tables were indeed cell phones. The men working the tables would pick one up, speak into it, then put it down. Two of them went through this robotic motion, while the other three huddled along a back wall. Two cars were parked to the side of the tables.

Danny's heart raced when he identified Victor Villa among the trio. "What are you doing out here?"

He debated getting another quarter-mile closer. From there, he might be in range to take a shot at Villa. The air was currently still. The sun beat down. Danny would have little to adjust to line up a long-distance shot.

As much as he preferred to get closer, they'd see his car.

Patience.

This was as good of a scenario as Danny would get to take out Villa. He'd been mentally planning for a one-against-thirty type situation at the compound. But one against five? You didn't need a mathematician to tell you how much better those odds were.

"Wait a minute." Danny pulled out his cell phone and opened the text message thread from Villa. He had yet to respond to anything the cartel boss sent, including the last message about having Sofia.

He typed his first response.

> When can you meet?

Danny pocketed his cell phone after confirming the message went through and returned to the binoculars. He watched as Villa stopped mid-conversation to walk toward the table nearest him, one that had only ten or so phones splayed out.

Villa grabbed a phone, read the message, and looked around at his companions. They all laughed. Villa rubbed the back of his neck before typing on the phone.

Seconds later, Danny's phone vibrated in his pocket. He read the new message.

READY TO MEET WHEN YOU ARE. YOU
KNOW WHERE TO GO. JUST TELL ME
WHEN.

Danny scouted the area surrounding this phone farm. He assumed all the phones were burners. But why have them all grouped together away from the compound?

Danny debated driving into the five men, but couldn't risk losing his only form of transportation. If he ended up stranded in this part of the desert, his survival wasn't guaranteed.

Danny returned to his car and dropped the binoculars on the driver's seat, grabbing his new AR instead. The vest was already strapped around his torso, complete with the three additional magazines full of ammo. One hundred and twenty rounds total, with more boxes in the car if needed.

But Danny wasn't coming back to the car. The ten dozen rounds would have to do.

He walked forward. Stealth was all he had right now. None of the men were walking around with guns like they did at the compound. They believed they were even further off the grid in this random location. Their relaxed nature suggested they had no worries about someone stumbling across their operation.

That's why you're out here. The phones are the heartbeat of communication between the cartel, its members, and anyone else involved in their operation. It's how Villa kept things going after the original raid when the compound had been abandoned.

Danny nearly broke into a sprint, moved by the thrill of closing in on Villa. The AR swayed from left to right with each step he took.

I can catch them by surprise. They'll be quick to respond, but if I can take out two before they realize what's happening, I'll have a real chance of getting out of here.

Death no longer weighed on Danny's mind. Only the success he'd long dreamed of.

He slowed to a walk once he was within one hundred yards of the tent. From the angle of his approach, the two vehicles blocked the cartel's view of him. All he had to do was stay low and move soundlessly.

When Danny was within fifty feet of a black Lincoln Continental parked behind a black Cadillac sedan, he squatted lower. He was close enough to hear the faint hum of the men's chatter. They laughed and howled. As he approached, the sounds of a party grew louder.

After the slowest, most careful steps he'd ever taken in his life, Danny pressed his back against the side of the Lincoln.

I'm here. And they don't have a clue.

He stood behind the back wheel to keep his feet from being seen underneath the Cadillac.

The men were speaking in Spanish, but he was still too far away to make out what they were saying. He thought he heard "Cortez" but couldn't confirm it. His heart was now pounding in his ears as the adrenaline bubbled up within.

Danny drew in a long breath, letting the warm desert air fill his lungs and bring clarity back to his rushing mind. He tiptoed toward the back of the Lincoln and looked around the corner.

Villa wasn't in his view. He was camped out toward the back of the canopy where a raggedy sheet hung to serve as a makeshift wall.

The two men tending to the tables full of phones were both visible, however, and neither of them looked in Danny's direction.

Take those two out, and Villa will come running to his car.

Danny silently dropped to a knee and got into a shooting position, the AR no longer an object, but an extension of his being. The trigger was cool beneath his finger.

He looked through the rifle's scope, lined up his shot. Only thirty feet away from his oblivious target. The man leaned back in his chair and crossed his hands behind his head.

A beautiful day to die.

With the man's face dead center in the crosshairs, Danny drew in one more breath, then pulled the trigger.

CHAPTER
THIRTY-ONE

THE MAN'S HEAD RUPTURED. Shards of skull and brain matter exploded. Blood misted the air.

Danny had the clearest view of the mess through his scope but couldn't dwell on the graphic scenery.

He swung his rifle around to the other man stationed behind a table, who had jumped out of his seat, and pulled the trigger again. The bullet caught him in the chest, which he clutched while writhing on the ground.

The three other men shouted, their boots clopping along the dirt in every direction. Danny remained on the side of the Lincoln, bracing himself.

Almost in unison, three other guns fired into the air. The men were shouting at each other. Most of it was lost on Danny, but he heard Villa command his men to find the shooter.

They knew Danny was close by. He didn't have a silencer on his AR.

The men fell silent, so Danny held his breath, listening for their approach. His heart hammered against his ribcage. His fingertips pulsed against the rifle's smooth surface with each heartbeat.

He heard the crunch of feet. Someone was right on the other

side of the Lincoln. Danny dropped low to peer under the SUV and found a man staring right back at him.

The man shrieked as his eyes widened. He waved his gun under the Lincoln and blasted several rounds toward Danny. But Danny had rolled back behind the wheel, covering his head with a free arm until the shower of bullets ceased moments later. The man hurt his own cause by popping several holes into the tire, which deflated instantly.

"He's behind the car!" the man shouted. The other man ran toward the Lincoln.

They're going to circle me.

Danny had to beat at least one of them to the punch. Since he was already toward the back of the vehicle, he jumped out from around the corner and pulled the trigger as rapidly as his index finger would allow.

His gamble had been correct.

The man who had locked eyes with him seconds ago now lay on the ground, face up, blood seeping out of half a dozen bullet holes across his chest and stomach.

Three down.

With each goon Danny killed, the more his confidence soared. He was now just one more kill away from having Villa one-on-one.

And to think I was ready to flee town.

Today's possibility of ending it all made Danny giddy. No more Villa. No more fake DEA holding his loved ones over his head. They could all go back to their normal lives.

He whirled around, expecting to see the other man coming from the front of the car, but no one was there.

Danny heard a sound from behind, spun, but too late.

A round hit him in the back, knocking him off balance. The vest stopped the bullet from killing him, but he lay face down, coughing up clumps of dirt.

He rolled over, squeezing the trigger of the AR, firing blindly.

The magazine emptied, and he swapped in the next one from

his vest. He didn't have the stopwatch he'd used at the hotel, but it had taken him under two seconds.

When he rose to his feet, no one was there. The canopy's cloth walls flapped in a light breeze. Danny discharged five rounds into the canopy.

"You missed," a voice called from the Cadillac parked in front.

The sound sent chills down Danny's spine. He hadn't heard that voice since the courtroom two years ago.

"Villa."

Danny spun around to see Villa standing behind the other man he'd been trying to shoot. He couldn't raise his AR, as the man already had his pistol fixed on Danny's face.

"Daniel Cortez," Villa said, stepping closer to his bodyguard. His face was practically on the man's shoulder.

Villa had aged in those brief years since Danny had last seen him. His head of thick black hair was now balding and stringy on the top, the sun gleaming off his scalp. He'd put on a few pounds but still had the devil in his eyes. Some things never changed.

Villa grinned, revealing yellowing teeth. He was clean-shaven after spending most of his life with a signature mustache. Danny understood, having shaved his own face to go unrecognized. But none of that mattered now.

"My good friend." Villa raised his arms in an embrace. "You found me. I can't say I'm surprised. That was always your best skill. Wish you could have worked for me. I have lots of things that need finding. Things that need hiding."

He's speaking to me like I'm already dead.

Despite being outnumbered and with a gun pointed at him, a strange calm blanketed Danny. He'd put up a good fight. Gave it the old college try. That sliver of hope pushed him far, but not quite to the finish line.

He took a small step backwards, still with his finger on the trigger, even with the AR pointed at the Lincoln to his left.

"Going somewhere?" Villa asked, cackling.

"This doesn't end here," Danny said. "You can't kill me."

Villa held his smile, a maniac expression that would haunt Danny's dreams. "And why is that?"

"I've been working with the DEA. They led me to this location. They're on their way. But I can stop them."

Villa laughed. "*Mentiras.* You're not with the DEA anymore. Even I know that. Don't you think I have people to give me that information?"

"Steele?"

Something flickered in Villa's eyes at the mention of Charles Steele. But Villa laughed. "I don't know what you're talking about. Too many hits to the head for you, amigo."

"You know damn well what I'm talking about. You thought you outsmarted me, but you failed again. I know Steele is working to keep the DEA off your trail. What he doesn't know is that I still have contacts in the DEA who haven't been compromised. They've been helping me, and they know where to come if they don't hear from me in the next hour."

"You're not making any sense." Villa grinned again, and Danny caught the doubt creeping onto his face. The smile was all a front. Villa hated what he was hearing.

"Call my bluff," Danny said, "but the people I'm working with aren't interested in playing by the rules. Not with the department hijacked by corruption. They will come in droves to your compound and burn it to the ground. They also know about what-ever the hell this place is. What are you doing out here, anyway?"

Villa shrugged. "Best cell reception in this part of the desert. Don't always get a signal at my house."

"What's it gonna be? Are you going to shoot me, or let me go? Whichever you decide, I prefer to get it over with quickly."

Villa peered into Danny's eyes from across the way. He was searching for any clue that might give away Danny's bluff. But Danny had played enough poker in his life. Being stared down didn't faze him. It had happened plenty of times with a month's salary riding on the bet.

Danny had no clue what would happen if Villa shot him dead in the desert. Maybe Zak *would* stir up a scene at the DEA offices.

Or maybe that's how my life ends. The rodents and vultures will be picking at my bones by sundown.

Villa was still glaring at Danny, his tongue between his lips.

He can't read me. And he hates it.

"Vamos," Villa finally said.

The man holding the pistol looked over his shoulder in confusion. Villa nodded at him, and he lowered his weapon.

Villa stepped in front of his guard and pointed at Danny. "This isn't over."

"I know it isn't," Danny said. "You still have Sofia. If you give her back to me, you'll never see me again. I'll let you be. Will tell the DEA I found your compound, but no one was there. They have no choice but to believe me."

Villa would never take such a deal, but Danny watched his opponent's reaction to see what he could get away with.

That horrid smile returned to Villa's face. "Sweet girl, that one. Really would be a shame if something happened to her."

Danny stepped forward, gripping the AR. "Where is she?"

Villa started backing away toward the Cadillac. His guard remained in place, finger also on the trigger and ready to react if Danny so much as sneezed. "Don't worry, she's safe. She's being fed. Has her own space."

The compound, of course.

But Sofia wouldn't be in the shed with the others. Villa would keep a close eye on her. Probably had her stowed away in one of the spare rooms in the house.

"Safe?" Danny asked. "Why should I believe that?"

Villa reached the Cadillac's passenger door, still grinning. "She's alive and well, and that's all that matters. Right? Unlike your friend, who I ordered to be killed after you locked me up. What was his name again?"

DANNY DRAGGED himself back to his car after Villa drove off in the Cadillac.

By the time he reached his own vehicle, tears filled his eyes, and a fire had ignited in his chest. Despite spending the last two years ignoring the obvious signs that suggested Dexter was dead—not to mention everyone who'd told him so—Villa squashed any lingering hope Danny had clung to.

What was his name?

Danny fumed at Villa's final words to him. It was Dexter who'd spoken on the witness stand for over an hour in his testimony against Villa.

Even hearing those cruel words from Villa didn't bring the closure Danny had long sought.

No. Revenge was perhaps the only thing that could quench his thirst. Villa walking around a free man, slimy and smug as ever, didn't sit right. The cartel boss wasn't entitled to a life of his choosing after ending so many others. That wasn't justice.

I want to be the last face he ever sees.

Danny turned the ignition and drove back to Las Cruces, growing angrier with each mile he drove. He thought of Dexter, whose corpse would be long gone by now. Danny had hoped to at least bring Dexter's body back for his family to bury. But Los Leones disposed of dead bodies in the desert where nobody would ever find them.

He thought of Sofia sitting terrified inside of Villa's house. Was she staring out a window, waiting for someone to rescue her? She was savvy enough to escape on her own but lacked the self-confidence to pull off such a feat.

Danny planned to see her soon and save both Sofia and Santiago from Villa's grip.

He thought of Nadia, trapped in an undisclosed location. All for doing the right thing by moving his mother to safety. Danny had been so consumed by Villa that he hadn't any rage left for the assholes pulling him in the other direction.

If he ever found out who was behind the secret text messages from the DEA, Danny would find them and squeeze their necks until their eyes popped out of their sockets. He'd become a pawn in their twisted game of corruption. He'd see to it they faced harsh consequences.

The only person Danny tried not to think of was his mother. If his thoughts wandered to her, he'd lose his focus. Few other people could sway Danny's emotions to the point of affecting his motivation.

Her failing health made his prospects grimmer. Had this same situation played out three years ago, Danny wouldn't have hesitated to sacrifice his own life to ensure his mother's safety. Now he had second thoughts.

How much time did his mom really have left? Doctors warned of how rapidly the dementia could accelerate. She could reach a point where, even if these DEA thugs kidnapped her, she wouldn't know what was going on.

The thought made Danny ill. Discounting his mother's life because she had only a little time remaining? Inhumane. Yet she'd be the first to tell him he'd be making a mistake to give up his life for an old lady in a retirement home. Not when the world could still benefit from his gifts.

While Danny refused to live in a world where people would threaten such harsh actions against that same old woman, he grew weary of fighting a constant uphill battle against the evil winning at every turn in his life.

When Danny finally arrived back at his hotel room, it was two o'clock in the afternoon.

The day had passed in a blur. Danny couldn't recall all the details that had led to him getting shot. He took off his vest and examined it under the desk lamp. The bullet was lodged in the thick padding. A nine millimeter.

That man had never intended to kill Danny. Not until Villa had ordered it. He could have easily shot Danny in the head.

Danny had long suspected Villa wouldn't kill him outright. The drug lord lusted for that face-to-face interaction with his future victims. He aroused himself from the psychological mind games he played. But Villa ran into a wall with Danny because Danny wasn't scared. Not of Villa. Not of dying in the middle of nowhere. Instead, Danny flipped the script and out-psyched the supposed criminal mastermind.

Villa got away, but the war still loomed. Danny had doubted his abilities until seeing those three men dead on the ground by his hands. He'd survived the one-on-five scenario, even if only because of a false narrative he pitched to Villa.

In the right situation, Danny now believed he could take on three of them at one time. He'd need to move fast, and he'd have to take out more than one at a time. Gambles lay in his future, and he'd keep doubling down until they no longer paid off.

He plucked the bullet out of the vest and tossed in the trash can. Looking into the bin, he spotted an old receipt from Enchanted Grounds, the coffee shop he and Sofia had visited several days earlier.

His heart sank. How dare they kidnap Sofia. She had nothing to do with any of this. She hadn't even attempted to break her brother free. All they had to do was let her leave Catalina, and that would have been the end.

Danny doubted she would have come back. She was too concerned about her friends and family to get further tangled in the mess, especially after they'd hung her innocent friend from the traffic light.

He had to make things right with Sofia. He admired her. She had invited him to run away with her, too. Start fresh elsewhere. That could only mean she liked him too. But now, too much damage had been done. Danny had failed to keep Dexter, Nadia, and his own mother safe. He had to break Sofia out of that compound to make things right.

And by going in, he could guarantee either himself or Villa would die, thus freeing Nadia and his mother. A win-win, right?

His phone vibrated with a new text message from the DEA posers.

> YOU HAVE UNTIL SUNSET TOMORROW
> NIGHT TO CAPTURE VILLA. IF YOU
> DON'T, NADIA WILL SUFFER.

They followed up the message with another picture of Nadia. She was still tied to a chair. Sweat glistened on every inch of her face. Her eyes were bloodshot. A bandanna tied around her mouth prevented her from speaking.

Just seeing her in that state made Danny's arms tremble.

Two women in dire straits all because of Danny. And they had no other options for rescue besides him.

> Where is she? Tell me, or I'll keep Villa for
> myself.

An hour passed without a response. They weren't going to. They were calling the shots. Danny could either capture Villa or face the consequences.

Villa wanted him dead. The DEA preferred him to suffer. Both roads were intersecting. With roughly over twenty-four hours to make something happen

The death toll would climb. Blood would spill in the desert.

Danny loaded his backpack with his Glock and a flashlight. He could no longer wait.

I need to talk to Murillo.

DANNY RELEASED Ramon Murillo after the man told him everything.

They'd spoken for an hour inside Sofia's shed, Danny holding his Glock ready the entire time. He took notes with his free hand while Murillo detailed everything from the names of individuals working in the compound, to their daily schedules and routes, and even those who had drama with each other.

Danny had no way of knowing how accurate the information was, but trusted Murillo had pure intentions of leaving the shed and returning to life outside the confined space. Danny pulled up a map of the area surrounding the compound on his phone and had Murillo pinpoint specific locations, like where vehicles entered and exited, the areas where security was heaviest, and what happened on different parts of the property.

Murillo didn't know for sure, but believed Sofia would be kept inside the house. When pressed for information on what Villa wanted with Sofia, Murillo only shrugged and said Villa loved using different people as pawns to get something bigger. He doubted Sofia would be harmed unless she defied him.

This eased Danny's nerves, but he still needed to bring the mess to a swift close.

The most critical piece of information Murillo provided was a location half a mile east of the compound. A lone rock hill stood elevated approximately one hundred and fifty feet above the ground. The top had a flat surface from which one could see the entire compound. Murillo assured Danny few people within the compound knew about the rock because they never traveled east—there were no roads.

But a few longtime cartel members who'd stuck around after Villa was sentenced knew of the secret location. In the past, they'd used it for undisclosed meetings out of Villa's sight. It was close enough for someone to stand guard and watch the activity unfolding in the compound.

It would be difficult, but taking out cartel members from half a mile away before storming the property would be Danny's best chance. Murillo estimated twenty-six full-time workers on the compound, but that included the man Danny had killed in the alley, and the men he'd wiped out at the burner phone farm.

That left twenty-two men standing between Danny and Villa.

After their talk, Danny walked Murillo into the front yard of Sofia's house and watched as he disappeared into the shadows of the night. He might regret the decision, but the men had a deal. And Danny had never reneged on his word.

The next morning, after staying up until midnight in front of his computer researching the compound and surrounding desert, Danny woke up at seven o'clock, ready for the day ahead. He'd saved onto his phone's hard drive all the images and screenshots of the maps he'd sketched, making a lack of cellular service a moot point once he reached the desert.

Danny drove east from Las Cruces, following the same route he'd taken the day before. He played no music and kept his mind clear. He'd made a rough schedule, but was ready to pivot if necessary.

His first stop was the phone farm. If Villa used everyone in his cartel as pawns, then Danny could do the same. He intended to scoop up all the phones. Murillo had explained how each cell phone had two names on the back. The first was the alias used by the caller, while the second was the sole person they'd contacted on that phone.

"Don Victor created a complicated network of burner phones with this method," Murillo had said. "It makes it impossible for anyone to trace the calls and activity. Villa drives out there to make calls so he doesn't have to use the same phone twice within a month. He's been extra cautious since he knows the feds are after him."

Danny didn't know why Murillo had shared such in-depth details about the phone farm, but understood when he arrived at his surveillance site. Looking through his binoculars, Danny noted three vehicles—the destroyed Lincoln was no longer present—and eight men marching around the tables. All of them carried guns this time.

"He set a trap," Danny said. "Well played, Murillo."

Danny couldn't approach the canopy with so many armed men, nor did he dare start shooting from a distance. Not with three vehicles that could chase him.

Villa was not with the group of men, so Danny pulled out his cell phone and sent a message back to the number Villa had texted him from. If what Murillo said was true, the odds of Villa holding that specific cell phone right now, wherever he was, were slim.

> I'm going to kill everyone inside unless you release the girl.

He sent the message along with one picture he had taken of the house in southern Catalina after following the cartel to their local hideout.

Danny returned to the binoculars and watched the action unfold. One man holstered his handgun and reached over a table to grab a cell phone. He read it, then called two other men over to show them the message.

That's got to be mine, Danny thought, riding sheer hope for his plan to work.

Another man grabbed a different phone and stepped aside to make a call. Danny presumed they were calling up the ladder for orders.

The men all huddled together, and a minute later, four of them broke off from the group and piled into the lone SUV. They sped out of the area, sending up clouds of dirt.

Danny cackled. "I can't believe that worked. Dumbasses."

His heart raced from the early success. Capturing more phones would make more moves possible. Ones he could use to direct the men where he wanted them to go—to their execution.

Four men remained under the canopy. If Danny could kill all four, that would leave eighteen men between Danny and Villa. The other four would be back once they discovered Danny's phony threat.

He grabbed his rifle and broke into a sprint toward the canopy, using the same approach as yesterday to creep up from the side where the vehicles blocked the men's view.

They stood close together, chatting and pointing at different phones on the table. Seeing their proximity made Danny run harder. If they stayed clustered together, his job would be easy.

He ran too fast. One of them heard his approach. The man looked over his shoulder, saw nothing because of the car impeding his view of Danny, then looked again and shouted.

Danny skidded to a stop about fifty yards away from the men and fired. He didn't need perfect accuracy. That was the beauty of a semi-automatic. He swept the barrel from left to right while pulling on the trigger with rapid, repetitive motions of his index finger.

The men pulled out their guns and shot back. Danny killed two before emptying his first magazine. A couple of rounds whizzed by his head, but the men didn't have a clean shot.

Danny slapped in a new magazine from his vest as he ran forward. The two surviving men rounded the vehicles. By the time they reached the other side, Danny had pulled the trigger ten more times.

The man on Danny's left flung up his arms as a round caught him. His pistol flew from his grip and sailed twenty feet behind him. Danny focused on the lone surviving man and blasted rounds in his direction until his magazine ran empty once more.

All four men were down. Danny gasped for breath as he ran toward the two nearest to him. At least thirty rounds had punctured the two vehicles, one Cadillac, one BMW. The Cadillac's two passenger-side tires were blown out.

The man on the right had collapsed instantly. Danny checked on him first. Blank eyes stared at the sky above. When his pupils made no movements after Danny stood over him, Danny kicked him in the arm to make sure he was dead weight.

The man on the left, however, twitched.

Danny raced over to find the man hanging on to the last threads of life. Blood dribbled from his trembling lips. His eyes saw through Danny, as if he were a pane of glass.

"Where did those men go?" Danny asked. "The ones who drove away."

The man grinned, revealing bloody teeth. "They'll be back."

His words were weak, garbled by a mouthful of blood.

Danny smiled back. "Guess I'll send them one more message."

He lined up the AR's sight with the man's forehead and pulled the trigger.

BETWEEN FOUR PANTS POCKETS, a protective vest, and his two God-given arms, Danny smuggled fourteen burner phones back to his car.

He tossed them onto the passenger seat, eyes wide as if he'd just robbed a bank.

Danny was far enough off the main road that he wasn't worried about being spotted by anyone who came to check on the farm, but he still needed to move quickly.

Sensing his own soaring confidence, Danny couldn't force himself to sit out the rest of the day.

That was too easy, he thought. *Easy is a trap.*

It would only be a matter of time before word spread that Danny faked a text message to send four cartel men on a ninety-minute drive to check on the house in Catalina.

Danny had shuffled the remaining phones around on the table to make it appear he had taken none. Fourteen out of nearly one hundred wasn't a big dent, but they'd find out eventually. That's why he needed to move fast.

Right now, they believed Danny sat outside the Catalina house. Someone had probably ordered the men there to scout the area.

Villa would have been alerted by now. Would he buy Danny's story?

Villa already had issues reading Danny. But the text message and accompanying picture couldn't be ignored. And wasn't that exactly what the cartel—and the DEA—had done? Send Danny pictures of his loved ones in peril to get him to act?

The cartel was down to eighteen men, but if Villa smelled danger, he'd call in reinforcements. And who knew how many extra men that could be.

Before Danny could continue, he needed to make a call.

He used one of the burner phones and dialed his mother's phone number. Part of him braced for someone else to answer. Someone who had kidnapped his mother and held her hostage until they got what they desired from Danny.

But the call went to voicemail, as it should. Danny had made sure part of the terms he'd created for Nadia when moving his mother included the need to turn off his mother's phone and leave it off.

No one could track her, even though it didn't matter now.

The robotic voice greeted Danny and prompted him to leave a message. After the tone, he drew in a deep breath and started speaking.

"Hi, Mom. It's me. I know a voicemail isn't the ideal way to hear from me."

The words poured out of Danny, and he choked back tears.

"Nadia moved you across the country because you were being targeted by dangerous men. As long as I'm alive, that may always be the case, but I couldn't sit back and do nothing. I had to leave Aspen immediately after learning Victor Villa escaped from prison. I had reason to believe he had his people watching you in that care facility.

"There's a good chance I'm going to die today. If I do, you'll get to live the rest of your days without worry. Both you and Nadia.

"I'm sorry for all the drama I've caused you, even if you never realized. Knowing how hard you worked to raise me always made me want to repay the favor. All I've wanted was to give you the life of your dreams. I've since learned you're not someone who ever had lofty dreams. You appreciated the simple things in life and never splurged on anything unnecessary. Except for that time you bought front row tickets to see Gloria Estefan in concert."

Danny laughed at the memory. It was the only moment he could remember his mother doing something enjoyable for herself.

"We may never speak again. So I wanted to tell you how much I love you. Don't ever think I'm going down without a fight. This may be the biggest punch I've ever thrown in my life. An evil man is tearing apart my life one piece at a time. He's doing the same to innocent people.

"I've made many mistakes, but because of you, I've grown to appreciate those mistakes as the moments that have shaped me. All credit goes to you, Mom. For the way I think, act, and believe. It all stems back to you.

"Do you remember when I made that book for you in elementary school? The one where you were the superhero who saved the boy from the monsters chasing him? This might sound silly, but I've never stopped believing in that story."

He released a shaking breath and cleared the emotion from his throat. "My life has been hard. I suppose when Dad died, it was always going to be hard. But you filled that void as best you could. All the times I got picked on, or beat up, it was you who came to save the day. And you did it all without ever showing a shred of hatred toward those who harmed me.

"You really are my hero. I still want to be like you when I grow up. If I could have just half as much self-confidence as you, my life would be completely different.

"My biggest mistake was letting Nadia go. You and I both know that. But you never once made me feel ashamed. All you did was provide comfort. I look back and think about all the small houses we bounced around when I was kid. But it was never about the house. A house is just four walls and a roof. *You* were my home. *You* were my warmth on the coldest nights. The shoulder to cry on in my darkest days. My cheerleader when I needed motivation.

"I know a lot of people try to claim their mother is their best friend. But you really are mine. You are the most selfless human being I've ever known. I only hope you can find peace in your remaining days knowing I tried."

Danny wiped the lone tear streaming down his cheek. "I'm going to kill a man, Ma. And he'll be ready for my arrival. You'll probably never know if I succeed or not, but just know that my last effort on this planet was to make the world a better place.

"I'm not sure what kind of news stories will come out about me, but all you need to know is that I was on the side of the good guys. In fact, I might be the only good guy in this whole mess."

Danny sighed.

"It's time for me to go. If I don't act soon, then all of this becomes your problem. I love you, Ma. Forever and always."

Danny hung up and stared at the phone. Villa was right about the reception being strongest in this remote location. Full bars.

He dropped the phone back into the pile with the others, then looked at himself in the rearview. His eyes were bloodshot and puffy. That call was the hardest he'd ever made, but it had to be done.

He scanned the area through his binoculars. The bodies still lay on the ground at the phone farm. No cars appeared from either direction.

With the maps saved on his phone, he pulled them open to find the best route to take to the secret rock. Five minutes between him and destiny.

Danny started his car and drove.

IT TOOK CAREFUL MANEUVERING, but after a ten-minute detour to avoid being spotted by anyone at the compound, Danny arrived at the rock.

Just seeing it sparked a fresh wave of hope. Murillo hadn't lied about the rock, after all. And the view it provided was even better than advertised.

Danny estimated he was much closer than a half mile out from the compound. Maybe a quarter mile. The rock acted as a ramp, simplifying his ascent as he lugged up his AR and backpack that now carried all fourteen stolen burner phones.

He looked through his binoculars. All activity within the compound walls reflected inside them. Five guards stood in front of the property gate, each one holding a rifle. There wasn't much action to see within the compound.

Danny spotted the shed that housed the lower-level, less permanent cartel thugs, at least two hundred feet away from the main gate. A couple of men walked together toward the house.

It wasn't quite a mansion, but Danny estimated the house ran around four thousand square feet. It was painted a pristine white with black trim and shutters. The roof, a reddish clay color, blended in with the colors of the desert from the point of view of the satellite cameras spinning around in space.

A handful of black vehicles were parked under a carport extending out from the west side of the house. Newly planted trees stood barren in front of the house. They tried, but nothing besides cactus and agave plants would grow in this part of the desert.

Danny studied the perimeter of the property, following the barbed wire fencing that created a confine slightly bigger than a football field. Random guards were stationed at different areas. Danny didn't think this was normal but instead part of Villa's heightened security after what happened at the phone farm.

He counted five other guards spread across the property, only two of whom were in a permanent position. The other three marched around in no apparent route.

"Ten guards." Danny shook his head.

He laid down, belly first, toward the edge of the rock, using the stuffed backpack as a makeshift stand for his rifle. He lay the rifle's muzzle over the backpack and peered at the compound through the scope. The zoom provided a more powerful view than the binoculars, as though Danny stood right inside the compound's fence.

He didn't have enough practice with long-range shooting to know how to adjust his shot based on the wind and trajectory. He'd use his first shot to gauge where his bullet would wind up.

The guards wore protective vests but no headgear. Danny moved the crosshairs from head to head, lining them up to land dead center. A breeze rustled over him, flapping the hem of his shirt sticking out beneath the vest.

Danny couldn't shoot and invite chaos so soon upon his arrival. He still had about thirty minutes before the men who'd left the phone farm would reach the house in Catalina. From there, how long would it be until they realized Danny was nowhere in town? That the whole thing had been a decoy?

Probably not until they returned to find the men slaughtered at the phone farm.

"Here goes nothing." Danny slid his rifle off the backpack and unzipped the bag to pull out a handful of cell phones. He had doubts his plan would work, but time was of the essence.

He spread out five phones in front of him and grabbed the first one. After clicking Contacts, he found the lone number stored and dialed it. The back of the phone indicated he was calling Ernesto, and that Danny was supposed to use the alias of Bill.

"Bueno," a man answered.

Danny's heart thumped violently. His throat nearly locked up with tension, but he got his next words out in time, forcing a slight Mexican accent. "Ernesto, it's Bill. Major problem at El Sombrero. Someone shot at the restaurant and now it's on fire. We need everyone there right now!"

"Wait, what?"

"Just get there now!" Danny hung up and grabbed the next phone. He delivered the same message to a man named Eddie. Then Steven. And finally, Gustavo and Ignacio.

They all shared the same reaction as Ernesto, questioning the details. But Danny reiterated the need for them to get to the taco shop immediately.

Murillo had admitted the network of burner phones was complicated on purpose. Danny hoped those complications only made it slower to get word back to Villa. He wondered if the men he had spoken to even recognized who was calling them. They could have just jumped into action based on the order. Would any of them contact Villa before heading out?

Danny had just pulled the pin from a virtual grenade. Now he'd see how the others reacted.

Still sprawled on his stomach, Danny returned to his binoculars to see the compound.

Two guards at the gate were now on their phones, rifles dangling at their sides. Another guard who had been roaming the property came running toward the gate with urgency.

An SUV zoomed out of the carport toward the gate, which the

guards slid open to let pass. Two of those guards climbed into the backseat of the SUV, which promptly sped away.

Danny had no idea how many people were in the SUV initially, so held his count at fifteen cartel members remaining in the compound.

He needed more gone, so took out another five phones and went through the same routine. One phone from the first batch started ringing. Danny rejected the call and stuffed the phones back into the backpack.

A second SUV steamrolled out from the carport, picking up another two guards at the gate before flying down the dirt road to head west toward Catalina.

Danny grinned. *It's actually working.*

They were down to twelve men on the property. No one had stepped out of the shed, so Danny presumed none of those dispensable criminals were currently on the property. Hell, they might have been some of the men he had spoken to.

Murillo had informed Danny that Villa sent those men to scout potential areas to expand their drug business. No cartel could operate without clients, after all. College campuses, shifty nightclubs, back alleys in the barrio. Nothing was off limits for Victor Villa. Money was money. Whether it came from a snobby trust-fund kid or a single mother battling addiction. It all counted the same.

Four men ran out of the house, but still no sign of Villa.

Two more phones rang from his backpack, and Danny could only laugh. All it would have taken was a phone call to the taco shop to confirm if there was a fire or not, yet these dummies just called *him* back.

Of the twelve presumed men in the compound, six stood together near the front gate in a huddle.

Danny's stomach churned with anxiety. This plan couldn't have worked any better.

He tossed the binoculars aside and replaced them with his AR-15. Through the scope, he observed the group of men bunched close together, shouting to each other. They all had looks of shock plastered across their faces.

He lined up a head shot on the man standing in the middle, figuring if the bullet swayed either way, it would still hit *someone*.

Right on his nose. He'll never see it coming. More chaos for them to sort out.

Danny drew in a deep breath, licked his lips, and blew out an exaggerated exhale. The world came to a stop as his finger tightened on the trigger. The breeze halted. Danny could taste the desert dirt in his mouth. He bit on his bottom lip, fighting to keep his trigger finger steady.

Before he pulled it, the sound of crunching footsteps came from behind him.

Danny froze, heart nearly leaping out of his throat.

"Finger off the trigger," a voice called from behind. Danny recognized it, but couldn't believe it. "Roll over and get up."

Danny did as instructed. When he rolled onto his back and sat up, he stared into the black hole of a revolver aimed at his face.

Holding the revolver, with hate in his eyes, was Ramon Murillo.

CHAPTER
THIRTY-SIX

THIS IS IT, Danny thought as he stared down the barrel of the gun.

Blood pumped uncontrollably through his veins as he stood up with his hands raised.

He had no clue what kind of man Murillo was. Could he be talked out of this situation? Bribed? Or was he hellbent on taking Villa the surprise gift of Danny's head?

"Not the sharpest knife in the drawer, are you?" Murillo said through gritted teeth. "I knew you wouldn't be able to resist the information I gave you. That's the only reason I told you the truth. Now here we are."

Danny gulped. His mouth had turned dry. "It doesn't have to end here."

Murillo laughed, keeping his revolver fixed on Danny. "You killed my partner, then locked me in a shed like some animal. What's stopping me from putting a bullet between your eyes right now?"

He's a talker.

Danny allowed a fragment of relief to creep back in. The more a man spoke, the less time he had for shooting. It wasn't an official motto of Danny's, but he had come to understand the sentiment after getting out of plenty of sticky situations in the past.

"You're right," Danny said. "That was harsh, and I should have handled it differently. But you have to understand the spot I was in. I'm getting threats to capture your boss or face torture for my mother."

Danny opted to leave Nadia out of the discussion. He wasn't even sure what to call her. His ex? Lover? Only hope for a bright future? Never mind Sofia. They'd have to figure out their relationship later, if she was open to it.

Murillo shook his head. "Bull. You're one of those feds who put Don Victor behind bars. Now you're out here trying to send him back."

"I was," Danny said. "But I'm not a fed anymore. Haven't been for years. It's actually the DEA threatening me to find Villa. They don't want to be involved at all and somehow think I'm the guy for the job."

"And you don't think you are?" Murillo's brown eyes looked Danny up and down. "You're here, right? What were you about to do if I hadn't shown up? Shoot all those guys? Then what?"

"I don't know," Danny lied. He couldn't openly confess the next phase in his plan was to stroll into the house and shoot Villa in the face. "I'm just kind of figuring things out as I go."

A phone rang inside the backpack.

"What's that?" Murillo demanded, gesturing to the backpack.

"Just my cell phone." Danny fought every urge to be a smart ass toward Murillo. But the gun pointed at his face did plenty of persuading. "Probably those DEA assholes trying to get a hold of me."

Danny threw out the lie to see what Murillo might know about the missing burners from their phone farm. He swung the revolver toward the backpack and fired three rounds.

The phone stopped ringing.

The air rippled as bullets flew past him. *He's not going to kill me. He would have done it by now.*

Danny considered each passing second a victory. He and Murillo had nothing to discuss, yet here they stood.

"Don Victor wants me to bring you to him," Murillo said. "He'll deal with you himself. Now, we can do this the easy way or the hard way. What will it be?"

Danny smiled. "I've always liked it rough."

He dove forward, staying low, and wrapped his arms around Murillo's knees. The two men tumbled down, Murillo's gun firing errantly into the distance. Danny drilled his fist into the inside of Murillo's forearm, forcing him to drop the weapon.

"Dammit!" Murillo shrieked, his hand flailing for the revolver now skittering down the rock.

Danny and Murillo were roughly the same size, Murillo having a slight advantage in the weight department.

Murillo swung his leg up and kicked Danny in the crotch.

Stars flashed in Danny's vision, blood rushing to his face as he grabbed the now throbbing area. A twisting sensation filled his insides, running up to his belly button and spreading down his thighs.

Murillo shoved Danny off and pivoted around to look for his revolver.

Despite the fierce pain in his crotch, Danny climbed to his feet, slightly off balance.

Murillo made the biggest mistake Danny could have asked for. He turned his back to find his weapon. Had the tables been turned, Danny would already have Murillo gasping for his last breaths. No gun necessary.

Danny grinned. *Some guys never learn how to fight. Relying on their little guns is all they know.*

He'd learned to fight after being picked on throughout elementary and middle school. The bullies called him an orphan. A

momma's boy. Danny later understood those were two contradic-
tory statements, but that hadn't mattered as a kid.

They'd follow him after school, pull him into an alley, and beat
the living daylights out of him.

Until one day, he'd fought back.

Aside from listening to Gloria Estefan, one of his mother's
hobbies had been watching Mexican boxing. She'd kept VHS tapes
with recordings of old fights from Julio Caesar Chavez, Ruben
Olivares, and Erik Morales.

Danny had studied these on the evenings he came home to an
empty house. Eventually, he'd learned to fight back.

As he watched Murillo scan the area for his gun, Danny thought
back to those bullies. They really were all the same in the end.

Murillo had drifted too far away, however. Danny was closer to
his AR than his nemesis. He spun around to scoop his rifle off the
rock. But Murillo, giving up on his gun, was all over Danny before
he could turn and fire.

Murillo used the same move Danny had, swiping at his forearm
with a balled fist, and knocking the rifle out of his grip.

The AR-15 soared off the miniature cliff and clattered to the
ground fifty feet below.

No time to dwell on losing his weapon. Danny grabbed his
backpack, full of fourteen shot-up cell phones and swung it by the
strap, his full weight behind it.

The bag connected with the side of Murillo's head. He grunted,
then fell to the ground. Murillo held his head with one hand, the
other flailing around. He kicked forcefully, catching Danny's knee,
which hyper-extended.

Danny wailed but continued forward. Murillo crouched, readying
himself. Danny swung the backpack around his head and let it fly.

The heap of cell phones smashed the other side of Murillo's
head. He spun around on a knee; his eyes rolled back into his head.
He fell backwards off the edge of the rock.

When the heavy thump sounded from the ground below, Danny scooted to the edge and looked down.

Murillo's limbs spread in every direction. And despite landing within three feet of Danny's rifle, he made no attempt to grab the weapon.

In fact, he made no movement at all. Judging by the way Murillo's neck was craned, how the back of his head was touching the front of his shoulder, it was surely broken. The fall had killed him.

"You should have shot me when you had the chance," Danny said, and spit over the edge.

With his knee, crotch, and forearm all throbbing in unison, Danny put the backpack over his shoulder and scrambled down the rock. A quick glance toward the compound showed no activity coming their way. The men, now only four of them, remained in their same positions. But the gunshot would have carried, and he couldn't chance someone coming out to investigate.

Murillo can be a decoy. Set him up in his car and shoot anyone who comes this way.

The idea invigorated him.

He hurried down the rock as best he could and rounded the base.

Murillo had arrived in a black BMW sedan, parked right behind Danny's vehicle.

When Danny reached Murillo on the ground, he was pleased to see he still hadn't moved. He kicked his AR out of the way and squatted down to pat Murillo's pockets.

He found a cell phone and pulled it out. It matched the other phones in his backpack, only this one had no labels on the back. That meant Murillo ranked higher and had a direct line to Villa.

Danny grabbed Murillo's dead hand and pressed his finger on the phone's sensor to unlock the screen. Once in, he went straight into the call log and text messages.

Six calls had been made back and forth between this phone and another unsaved number within the last hour. Danny tapped on the number to view any text messages between the two phones.

It was definitely Villa.

> Bring the little fed boy to me. He needs to learn a lesson. Some suffering and a bullet to the head should do the trick.

Murillo only responded with a thumbs up. Nowhere in the messages had Murillo said where Danny would be. But Danny didn't know what they had discussed on their calls.

Villa might send someone out to this rock any moment now, and Danny needed to be ready for his rushed plan.

He grabbed Murillo by the ankles and pulled him toward his car.

DANNY FOUND a lot more than he'd bargained for in Murillo's car. The sun blasted as it moved west, sweat making his shirt cling to his back.

When he reached the vehicle, he popped the trunk to find rope. He intended to use it to prop Murillo up by tying his body and head to the driver's seat.

A rope lay on top of two wooden crates in the trunk. One crate housed ten handguns, five grenades, and a protective vest. The other contained at least three dozen sticks of dynamite.

Danny whistled when he found this hidden treasure, running his fingers along the crate's surface. He'd never seen a bomb in person but had studied their construction and effects as part of his DEA training.

He looked at Murillo's dead body lying at the side of the car. "Were you planning on blowing something up?"

Danny's internal clock kept ticking, but he'd forgotten all about his worry of someone coming to find him at the rock. If anyone did, Danny had an upper hand in the weapons department. He hadn't seen anyone in the cartel ever toss a hand grenade, and he now had five at his disposal.

"We're gonna change up the plan, Murillo. I have a much better idea for how to use you. If you don't mind, of course."

Danny grabbed the rope he'd initially sought, then closed the trunk's lid to conceal his new stockpile.

Instead of pulling Murillo into the driver's seat, Danny dragged him around the car and let him ride shotgun. He returned to the site of the fall and retrieved his AR-15 and backpack.

After tossing those on the middle console, Danny hopped behind the BMW's wheel and drove away from the rock.

To stay out of sight from the compound, Danny looped around the property, keeping a mile radius. It was tedious driving over the off-road desert, but the car did just fine at a lower speed.

When he finally reached the main dirt road that led into the compound, still a mile away, Danny parked the car.

He looked over at Murillo. "What do you say? Not much, I suppose. But it's time, my friend. I'm not going to let you die without good reason. You can help me save innocent people. Blink twice if you disagree."

Danny cackled at himself, wondering if he'd lost his marbles.

After checking the road behind him and assured that no one approached from the east, Danny tossed his bag and rifle in the backseat, opened the door, and pulled Murillo over the center console.

It was much harder to yank the dead weight within the confines of the car. The body wasn't as flexible as Danny had thought it would be. He spent a couple minutes bending each of Murillo's limbs to get him properly seated in the driver's seat.

Danny didn't need as much rope as he'd thought. By reclining the seat at a slight angle, Murillo's body didn't slump over the steering wheel. Then he used the rope to tie Murillo's hands to the steering wheel, and his head to the seat's headrest. This also kept the body from tipping to the left or right.

Danny flipped open the center console compartment and found a pair of sunglasses. He promptly slipped them onto Murillo's face.

"Looking good, sir." Danny stepped back and admired his handy work. Murillo's hands were low enough on the steering wheel that anyone looking wouldn't see the ropes holding them in place. It also helped that the side windows were tinted almost pitch black.

The only decent view into the vehicle was through the windshield. From Danny's test, Murillo appeared to drive the car himself.

Satisfied with the first step of his plan, Danny popped open the trunk and brought the crate of dynamite to the passenger seat. He grabbed all the handguns and stuffed them around the dynamite crate and along the sides of Murillo's body.

He kept the grenades for himself—dumping out the damaged cell phones into the backseat—and stuffed them into his backpack.

With his AR-15, five grenades, and half of the cartel in a manufactured panic, Danny knew the next few hours would determine success or failure. Life or death. The longer he waited, the more cartel members would return to the compound.

He drew a deep breath and reigned in his racing thoughts. He tended to get ahead of himself and now he needed discipline. He leaned over Murillo, started the car, and put the BMW in drive.

The car crept along at four miles per hour. Danny stayed sandwiched between the open driver's door and the inside, reaching in to control the steering wheel. He kept the car on the dirt road, often checking behind him to make sure no one else was coming and looking ahead to ensure he wasn't too close to the compound.

It took seven minutes to move a quarter mile, a steady walk for Danny. Fresh sweat broke out around his crown. A couple vultures flew overhead, smelling the fresh food waiting for them in the BMW.

If all went according to plan, those poor vultures would have to seek their meal elsewhere.

Three minutes later, they were an eighth of a mile out from the compound. Danny had done some testing, letting his hands off the steering wheel for stretches, and found the car had rather sound alignment. It pulled slightly to the right, but at their dragging speed, he didn't expect this to cause problems.

Just one more factor to account for.

Getting too close for comfort, Danny reached in and put the car into neutral, bringing it to a complete stop after it crawled another thirty feet.

"It's go time, my friend." Danny removed the lid from the crate of dynamite and tossed it in the backseat. He angled the steering wheel to the left to account for the alignment. "Godspeed, amigo."

Danny put the car back into drive, slammed the door, and gave the car a gentle push. The BMW crept onward.

A quarter mile was a little over thirteen hundred feet. Once the car was within one thousand feet of the front gates, the guards would see it. He ventured to the far right of the road, approaching the towering fence that secured the compound perimeter.

No other guards patrolled the area beyond the front gate, leaving Danny plenty of space unobserved. He didn't know for sure how far he could throw a grenade, but judging by its shape and weight, he estimated he could toss it at least eighty feet. Assuming it would roll another ten or twenty, Danny needed to get within one hundred feet of the front gates to execute his plan.

The alignment of the steering wheel worked to perfection. Over the next three hundred feet, the BMW crept toward the left side of the road before beginning its return to the center. It stayed centered for the next two hundred feet, leaving five hundred more to reach the front gates.

Danny reached the fence and crouched low, keeping a pace of roughly five car lengths behind the coasting BMW.

Voices shouted from up ahead, but they were too far for Danny to make out their words.

The fence cast a weak shadow over Danny. Not only did it keep him cool, but it also kept him out of sight from the guards ahead. Granted, all they'd have to do was look in his direction to see him, but their attention was drawn to the car creeping toward them.

Two hundred feet to go. Danny's limbs trembled. The adrenaline improved his vision and focus. He hadn't factored that into the equation and now believed he could throw the grenade farther than originally planned.

Six guards stood outside the gate now, each with their rifle drawn and aimed at the BMW. Their shouting continued in Spanish, demanding the man in the vehicle identify himself.

Danny grinned. This couldn't have worked better.

The car was within one hundred feet of the gate, and the guards' demands grew louder. Danny heard the desperation in their shouting toward the dead man behind the wheel.

He watched as the car crept closer to the gate, within fifty feet. Two guards ran out from the gate and dropped to a knee for a better shooting position.

Danny stopped about a hundred feet from the gate. He could see the guards as clearly as they'd looked through his scope earlier. He took off his pack and pressed his back against the fence while fishing out a grenade.

The two positioned guards opened fire on the BMW, the symphony of gunshots sounding in the otherwise still desert.

Danny's heart sank. He didn't think they would shoot the BMW, considering it belonged to one of their own. If a bullet hit the crate of dynamite, it could create enough friction to ignite the bombs too soon.

When the car didn't stop upon reaching the gates, the two guards who had shot the vehicle jumped to their feet and sprinted to each side of the rolling BMW. They pulled open the doors, sticking their rifles in first, then quickly retreated when they found no active threat.

The guard on the passenger side waved the other guards over, and that's when Danny dashed thirty feet ahead. He stopped, planted his feet, and pulled the pin from the grenade.

His knowledge of grenades was limited to what he'd learned in DEA training. Simple devices. Pull the pin, throw, get the hell out of Dodge.

Danny reared back and watched the grenade sail through the air. Adrenaline provided him extra strength and force. He couldn't have executed such a perfect throw if given another hundred attempts, but the current toss was the only one that mattered.

The grenade hit the ground about twenty-five feet short of the BMW, then rolled end over end toward the car. The guards all whipped their heads around at the sound. Two of them shouted. A third jumped out of the way.

The grenade detonated, rumbling the ground all the way to Danny's position some thirty yards away. The explosion rocked the car.

A split second later, the entire BMW ruptured as the dynamite inside exploded. The car itself became a grenade, scraps of metal and shrapnel flying in every direction. A tire rolled past Danny with no signs of slowing.

All six guards lay dead on the ground, surrounding the BMW's carcass. Smoke filled the sky, casting a gray cloud over the compound.

More voices shouted from within the house. Danny peered through the fence to see another six men running from the front porch, rifles held at the ready as they sprinted toward the gate.

Danny reached into the backpack and pulled another grenade. He broke into a mad dash toward the gate. The last twenty feet of the fence abutted the brick wall that held the swinging steel gates in place.

He stopped at the corner of that wall, rifle fire turning the bricks into stinging shrapnel around him. Danny listened to footsteps pounding closer. When he guessed they were within fifty feet of the gate, he pulled the pin from another grenade and rolled it around the brick wall toward the charging men.

All six guards skidded to a halt, dirt flying from their heels. One slid and covered his head, but the others were fully exposed when the grenade detonated. Shielded by the brick wall, Danny jumped out from behind his hiding spot and opened fire on anyone still moving.

Three guards were already dead and the other three writhed on the ground, trying to crawl back to the house.

Danny planted a round in each of their backs, then three more. For good measure. The metallic scent of blood clashed with the burning metal from the grenades and the BMW.

Success never smelled so sweet.

Danny stepped over the dead bodies, running through the numbers in his head. Twelve dead henchmen all outside. If his calculations were correct, there would be no other guards to come save Villa. Not until the ones who had been sent on a false mission returned.

But by then, Danny expected to be done with what he'd come here for.

He loaded a new magazine into his AR and started for the house, where Victor Villa waited with no protection.

CHAPTER
THIRTY-EIGHT

DANNY STOPPED JUST outside the front door and listened.

Silence.

He expected more men to barge out, but none came. Somewhere inside, Villa waited. After seeing what Danny had just accomplished, the cartel boss wouldn't take any chances. Especially not with a gimp shoulder.

Danny had every advantage in the book, aside from knowing the layout inside Villa's house. He'd seen some blueprints of the place after Villa's capture, but he hadn't memorized them, assuming he'd never step foot in New Mexico again.

He looked back over his shoulder at the destruction he'd caused and grinned. Ramon Murillo had been the lifeline Danny didn't know he'd needed. From the useful information Murillo disclosed, to the surprise gifts of his dead body and trunk full of explosives. None of this was possible without Murillo and his thirst for revenge.

And to think he could have been the one Danny had shot in the alley. Sometimes destiny dealt you the exact cards you needed. But Danny wouldn't count on his lucky streak continuing.

After two minutes in front of the house, Danny climbed up the three short steps of the wooden porch. The set up was one his mother had always dreamed of. A swing hung on his right. To the left stood a table with two chairs and a chess board.

Villa had made all the right moves yet faced a checkmate.

Danny approached the door and rapped his rifle's muzzle against the wooden surface. He would still be polite, no matter how many people the man inside had murdered.

When no one answered, Danny twisted the doorknob and pushed. The door creaked open to reveal the interior of the residence of an obnoxiously wealthy man. High vaulted ceilings with two gaudy chandeliers dangling above. Paintings decorated the walls. Danny calculated the astronomical value of the abstract portraits.

A living room was arranged on the right side of the house. Two couches centered around a television tucked into the corner. Through the living room was the kitchen, abandoned except for a couple of dishes in the sink. The dining table appeared immaculate.

Danny didn't venture into any of these rooms, instead traversing down the hallway that led to the back of the house. Villa was a coward, and Danny didn't need any evidence to know he was hiding, hoping to lure him into a trap.

"Don Victor," Danny shouted. "Are you okay?"

Silence.

It was worth a try.

The hallway had three doors. Danny approached the first and found the bathroom. After a quick check behind the shower curtain, he returned to the hallway and tried the next door.

Villa's bedroom.

A box of cigars and an ashtray sat on his nightstand next to a pile of magazines ranging from sports issues to nudies. The bed was made, nothing but a suit jacket lying across the top blanket.

"Don Victor," Danny tried again.

The old man might have thought someone from Catalina had

come to rescue him. Danny looked up and encountered a camera watching him from the corner of the ceiling.

Danny craned his neck, then fired two rounds. The camera exploded into shards. Wherever Villa hid, he was surely watching Danny's every move.

"Sofia?" he called out. If Villa wouldn't respond, maybe Sofia would.

But Danny didn't sense anyone present in the house. He left the bedroom and proceeded to the last door at the end of the hallway. Behind it, he found Villa's office.

A desk sat beneath the window overlooking the south side of the property. A lone laptop lay closed on the surface. A bookshelf contained several books.

"Come out and play!" Danny shouted when he spotted the camera in the office. Then he shot it down.

Where the hell is he?

Danny had checked all the rooms in the house, yet it appeared no one had been inside at any point today. He wondered if the house really had been abandoned when the DEA had come to clear out the place after arresting Villa. He'd only been out of prison for a few days, but it appeared the property had been maintained as if nothing had happened.

He peeked back out into the hallway to make sure no one was sneaking up on him. With the house having only one level, Danny lowered his rifle and placed his hands on his hips.

He looked around the office. Neat piles of papers and files stood on the polished desk. A laptop sat closed. A desk organizer contained all the other office supplies one needed.

Had Villa been in one of those vehicles that had sped out of the compound? Maybe he sensed the hot water coming his way and fled his home. But why would he have left all those guards behind?

Danny looked down at the floor, studying the designs on the rug beneath the rolling office chair. It had the typical southwestern patterns he'd become used to seeing all over the great state of New Mexico.

Under the desk, the rug's corner curled upward. An odd place for a curve in the fabric. It wasn't near where a person's feet might have fidgeted beneath the desk, nor was it near any of the desk's legs.

Danny squatted under the desk to examine it more closely. He pulled at the corner, and as the rug receded, he found a trap door in the floor.

That's more like it.

Danny cleared the rug completely from the floor and tossed it into the hallway. He moved silently across the hardwood, gripping his rifle, knowing he still had twenty-eight rounds loaded in the magazine.

A grenade would have been perfect to toss down the trapdoor, but he didn't know if Sofia was down there. Or any other innocent people tangled up in this mess.

Danny had no choice but to gamble. Lift the door and pray a slug to the face didn't greet him. He dropped to a knee and readied his rifle in his right hand while pulling up the door with his left.

The hinges groaned as he opened it and relief flooded him when he found no one staring back. Instead, a short ladder running along a concrete column invited him to climb down to a concrete floor about ten feet below.

He's down there. And he's not coming up. This has to end in his little bunker. Didn't Hitler die in a bunker?

All cowards were the same in Danny's book. He twisted his body and climbed down the first three rungs on the ladder.

That reduced his fall to roughly seven feet, so Danny let go and landed with a sharp thud on the ground. The concrete floor sent jolts of pain up to his knees, but he rose to his feet and stared into the eyes of Victor Villa.

Danny spotted the pistol in Villa's hand and dove to his right.

Villa fired. The shot missed, sending shards of concrete flying from the wall behind Danny.

He shot four more times, Danny dodging and jumping in different directions to avoid contact. One shot whizzed by his ear.

After another, Villa stopped to reload. Danny fired in Villa's direction.

Nothing landed. Villa had dodged behind a desk, then dashed toward the corner of the room.

Danny surveyed the area. The bunker was nearly as big as the house, spanning almost two hundred feet. The long side of the room was a wall of screens with camera feeds from all around the property.

The cartel boss broke into a hobbled dash toward them.

Danny watched the old man crash into the panels controlling the screens then whirl around holding a Tommy gun.

Villa unleashed a flurry of shots, drawing a near perfect line in the wall behind Danny, who sprinted in zigzags back to the ladder behind the concrete column.

The shower of gunfire ceased, and Villa cackled with mad delight. "Daniel Cortez in my house! I never dreamed of the day!"

I really have him one-on-one. If anyone else shows up, I can shoot them as they come through the trapdoor.

The adrenaline helping him dodge bullets hadn't waned. Danny could taste the finish line. He just needed to execute.

Villa fired off another series of shots. Too many to count. Maybe a couple dozen. Some Tommy guns had drum magazines that could hold a hundred rounds. Maybe more.

"Where's Sofia?" Danny shouted around the corner, sticking his face out for a split second to see where Villa was.

He was still hanging out by the monitors.

Villa laughed. "She's still alive. Might be the only one you didn't kill with your grenades. Impressive, by the way. I've always said you'd make a great addition to my team."

"Where is she?!"

Villa howled. "You think this is the only bunker on the property? What do you think all the explosives are for?"

He's not going to tell me.

"We can still make a deal," Villa continued. "I let the girl go free, and you let me walk out of here. I promise you'll never see me again. Already have a place ready in Mexico. Can have a chopper here in thirty minutes."

"Why would I let you go after all of this?" Danny shouted back.

"Mercy, amigo. Mercy. I don't have many years left. Don't make me spend them in a prison."

Don't make me?

Was Villa conceding defeat?

Danny dropped to a knee and tightened his finger around the rifle's trigger.

"The call is ultimately yours," Villa said. "I've been trying to make a deal with you this entire time, but we can't seem to come to terms."

"My only term is that you get the justice you deserve."

Danny lunged out from behind the wall and squeezed the trigger as fast as he could.

Villa returned fire. The bunker erupted in the deafening cacophony of gunshots. A round hit Danny in the ankle. He dropped to the floor behind the corner, biting down on a scream from the burning pain.

The room fell silent. Villa was no longer chirping or shooting. The stench of gunpowder filled the room. Danny peeked around the corner. Saw Villa lying on his back. He couldn't tell if the man's chest rose or not. But Villa was down, and the Tommy gun lay just out of reach.

Danny fumbled in his pockets to pull out his cell phone and dialed Zak. The screen grew blurry, showing one bar of signal.

Please go through.

Zak answered while Danny's head swum in another dimension. He glanced down and saw blood spurting from his ankle. Nausea swept over him. Shock from blood loss.

"I'm losing blood," Danny mumbled, consciousness fading. "Got Villa. At compound. Send help."

WHEN DANNY WOKE thirty minutes later, he found the bunker exactly as it had been when he'd passed out.

Villa lay in the same spot but had rolled on to his side. The Tommy gun remained untouched.

Danny's head spun. When he sat up, he grabbed the wall next to him until the dizziness passed. Shock, fatigue, and dehydration, all combined in a sickening cocktail throughout his body. His ankle had stopped bleeding, the residue soaking his sock and pants leg, now stuck to his flesh. The pain still throbbed, a muted sensation.

The open doorway in the ceiling let beams of light shine down.

Jesus. Going through that house was a lifetime ago.

Danny flexed his foot to see how bad the pain in his ankle really was. He'd sprained his ankle plenty of times as a kid, running through the dirt fields near his house. This pain, however, was a steady throb that heightened with every subtle movement.

A bullet wound to the ankle would take weeks, if not months, to fully recover from. That was time he was more than happy to take for himself. After visiting his mother, of course. And Nadia, if she'd allow it.

Danny used the wall to help himself rise from the dusty

concrete floor. All weight had to go on his good ankle, and he hobbled toward Villa.

He expected to find his nemesis unconscious and almost jumped back when he got within three feet and caught Villa's hateful, brown eyes spring open.

Villa had dried blood near his already damaged shoulder, and another stream of still moist crimson oozing from his stomach. His cracked lips parted into his signature manic grin.

"Here we are," Villa said, his voice hoarse. "You crazy son of a bitch. Did you really pull this off by yourself?"

Danny staggered to the left, wincing with each movement, and squatted down to grab the Tommy gun to toss it further from Villa.

Checkmate, amigo.

"I had my doubts," Danny said, wincing as he lowered himself to one knee to ease the throbbing pain in his ankle. "I understood the odds I was up against. But I figured as long as either you or I got killed today, then at least my loved ones would be safe."

"Such a noble man. Fearless when staring death in the eye. I completely understand. You outplayed me, Cortez. Again. Let's get this over with. I prefer quick and sweet, if you're taking requests. A bullet to the head will suffice."

Danny returned a grin. "I'm not going to kill you. I'd prefer you rot in a prison cell for the rest of your miserable life. And after an escape from Florence, I'm willing to bet most of your days will be spent in solitary confinement. You'll go mad in there. They'll break you. And I hope when you're grasping at that final shred of sanity, in that moment before you know they've won, you'll think of me."

Villa's eyes widened, and that was all the proof Danny needed to know he'd made the right decision.

Danny rose from his knee and turned around, taking extra caution to avoid causing more pain to shoot up his leg.

He walked away as Villa made a choking sound, a garbled laugh. Danny turned around to see that crazed look in Villa's eyes.

"You really don't know what's going on, do you?" Villa asked, a painful smile stuck on his face. "I'll be damned. Here I was, thinking you were playing dumb the whole time."

Danny raised an eyebrow. "What do you mean?"

"I won't be in solitary for long. Someone will kill me along the way."

"Who?"

"The DEA. That's why I thought you were playing dumb. Maybe they brought you out of retirement to work undercover. But you're just here on your own accord. At least, in the beginning, right?"

Danny's face scrunched as confusion swept over him. "The DEA wants you dead? Why would they care if they've already locked you up in the first place?"

Villa's smile widened. "I understand your confusion, Cortez. I'm Victor Villa, the big, bad cartel boss, right? Well, that's a complete lie. I'm just a middleman like anyone else in the American drug ring. Who do you think helped me escape prison?"

"Why would the DEA help you get out of prison?"

"To kill me, of course. They tried plenty of times while I was in there. Most fights get broken up, but not if I was the punching bag. They'd let it go until I was left bleeding and unconscious. But they didn't know who they were attacking. I don't just die. They would leave rope for me some nights, little razor blades. I'm no dummy. You think I'd give them the satisfaction of doing their dirty work for them?"

"Why help you escape, though?" Danny asked. "They could have kept cranking up the heat in the prison. Maybe a guard would have shot you and they could've made up a story."

Villa nodded, color slipping out of his face as he continued bleeding from his stomach. "That's the happy ending we all would have preferred, right? The DEA grew tired of me because I was still cutting into their profits. Even while I was in prison. I didn't go into that hellhole without a plan to keep the business afloat. See, they thought locking me up would give them free reign over my territories.

"But they were met with swift and harsh resistance. The day I checked out of the prison hospital, two guards directed me to a hallway I'd never seen. At the end of it was a door leading to the outside. All the guards in the tower conveniently had their backs to me as I walked right off the premises."

"So you never staged your escape? We all thought you planned it and had someone waiting to pick you up."

"I had a plan in the works, sure. It was going to take some time. Building tunnels and all that. But it never came to that. I ran as far as I could and hid between bushes for two days, waiting for the helicopters to stop flying overhead. I knew they would shoot me the second they saw me. It was all theatrics, see? An escaped convict on the run. No one would bat an eye if they shot me dead in the middle of the street."

"So, who's been messaging me from the DEA?" Danny asked. He forgot all about his wound and the pain.

"Probably the same people who want me dead. You see, Cortez, the DEA are the true drug lords here. Yes, they make their busts, haul away the drugs and money. But it's all for appearances. Where do you think those drugs and money go? To the government? Back to the taxpayer? They go right back into the same marketplace, just somewhere else."

Danny refused to believe a single word Villa spoke, but the delivery was convincing. Besides, why would Villa make all this up moments before he was to be hauled back to prison? "The DEA doesn't deal drugs. I've worked there. I know people from the bottom all the way to the top."

"Who knows better about how a drug cartel operates than them?" Villa said. "They know how to bust them, which means they know how to hide them. I'm not the first victim to fall prey to their greed. This is what they do. Find the cartels. Throw their leader in prison. Then watch as the organization crumbles so they can swoop in and claim everything as theirs. The world is a crooked place, Cortez. I'd have thought you'd know that by now."

Danny rubbed his forehead. Why *did* he have only one contact in the DEA after befriending several dozen colleagues? He'd had his trust issues with the department, but always believed it was because of bureaucratic matters. Maybe the answers had always been in front of him.

His head and body turned hot and heavy.

Sirens sounded in the distance, their wailing heard all the way down in the bunker.

"You can still finish this yourself," Villa said. His eyes grew droopy and bloodshot, flesh becoming paler with each passing second. Danny wasn't sure Villa would survive a trip in the ambulance to the nearest hospital anyway, assuming an ambulance was even coming.

"If everything you said is true, then there's no reason for me to have your blood on my conscience." Danny looked his nemesis in the eyes one last time. "The world will take care of you as it sees fit."

Danny turned, hobbled away, and labored up the ladder to freedom.

CHAPTER
FORTY

DANNY SAT on the swing on Villa's front porch, watching the clouds of dust that trailed behind the dozen vehicles speeding toward the property, sirens blaring and lights flashing.

To Danny's surprise, the vehicles were mostly FBI, with a couple of police cars from Las Cruces.

Danny stood and raised his arms as the fleet screeched to a stop in front of the porch. A handful of FBI agents drew their guns and trained them on Danny until they were ordered to back down and go into the house.

The man who shouted the order strolled over to Danny and extended a hand to shake. "Danny Cortez?"

Danny had met plenty of people during his time with the DEA, but didn't recognize this guy. He was around the same age but looked older thanks to the bags under his eyes and gray hairs taking over the sides of his head.

"Yes." Danny returned the handshake.

"I'm Special Agent Michael Green. Let's talk somewhere more private." The FBI agent walked past Danny to the side of the house, making him limp over. When he spotted the blood from Danny's ankle, his eyes widened. "My apologies. An ambulance should be here soon. They'll get that cleaned up."

Danny ignored Green's concern for his ankle. "How did you know my name?"

"That's why I wanted to talk in private," Green said. "I'm a friend of Zak's. He contacted me when you first reached out to him. We've actually been in town for the past week trying to find something to pin on this cartel. Keeping things secret from the DEA has been the hardest part. We've had our suspicions about the department for a while now."

Danny shook his head. "Hold on. You've known about the DEA?"

Green raised his thick hand. "I said we had *suspicions*. We need proof the DEA has corruption. It's a heavy accusation to make against an entire government agency and shouldn't be treated lightly."

"So, did you find anything?"

Green nodded. "Not regarding the DEA corruption. But on the cartel, yes. We found a site seven miles east of here with two dozen dead bodies. Our team has been working on that site all week."

"Why are you telling me all this?" Danny asked. "Isn't this an open investigation."

"It is. And normally I wouldn't say a word. But I'm counting on your testimony to help throw this entire cartel behind bars. I'll share what I can about this investigation, in confidence. And you'll share with me. But that's for another time. Zak told me about your old partner. Found something you might want."

Green reached into his coat pocket and pulled out a small black booklet. Danny flipped it open to find the familiar golden badge with an eagle hovering above the emblem of the United States Drug Enforcement Administration on the right-hand side. On the left, though tattered and dirty, was Dexter's DEA identification card. His portrait smiled at Danny.

"Sorry for the bad news, Mr. Cortez. But your partner's remains were found among the bodies recovered. Forensics will confirm which remains belong to him, and we'll arrange delivery to his family."

Danny opened his mouth but couldn't speak. The closure he'd long been chasing finally came, yet he didn't feel any better. "I can keep the badge?"

Green shrugged. "It's against protocol. But I've lost a partner before, too. I know how it is. Just keep this our secret and we won't have any problems."

A tear streamed down Danny's face. Dex was gone. Officially confirmed. But getting to hold something that once belonged to his old partner caught him off guard. He'd never expected such an honor.

"Were you aware of the cartel hiding in Catalina?" Danny asked to shift the focus back to Los Leones. He slipped Dex's badge into his pocket.

"Thanks to you, yes. We've been monitoring your phone activity. We made twelve arrests this morning and believe any cartel member hiding in Catalina has been accounted for. More are hiding in Las Cruces. We have a team out there still searching for them."

"Do you know if Santiago Hernandez was one of the arrested?"

Green nodded. "Yes, he was."

"For what it's worth," Danny said, "he was working for the cartel against his will. They were blackmailing him by threatening his sister, who ended up being kidnapped. I thought I'd find her here but haven't seen anyone."

"He'll get to share his side of the story, but his fate will be up to the courts. Now, I have some other matters to address. Zak is an incredible friend, by the way. The things he went through to get information and relay it to me, all while knowing the risks of losing his job. Wow, is all I can say."

"Don't tell me he lost his job."

Green shook his head. "Not as of now. And thank God. I need him on the inside if we have any hope of rooting out the corruption in the DEA. We'll do some digging into the number that's been texting you. Even though they claimed to be with the DEA, I don't believe they actually are. Tough to say. Anyway, the first matter. We found your Nadia Binetti. She was being held in an old warehouse in Syracuse. The place was abandoned, so we believe whoever was holding her there knew we were coming. Nadia sent a message to you."

Green pulled out a notepad and handed it over to Danny.

I'm safe but will never forgive you. I need time before speaking to you again. Your mom is in an assisted living facility in Watertown, NY. Good luck with everything.

Danny handed the notepad back to Green, who had an awkward smirk on his face. Before Danny could say anything, Green spoke again. "We checked on your mother—Nadia let us know her alias. She is fine and well in her new home."

"Thank you for doing that, I—"

"Danny!" a voice shouted from across the front yard.

Both men turned around to look. Running from the shed that he believed housed the overflow cartel thugs was Sofia. She sprinted to Danny, sweat soaking her clothing. Her hair was frazzled, her eyes bloodshot.

Danny stood as she pounded up the porch steps and threw her arms around him, pressing her lips forcefully against his. After getting through the salty flavor of the sweat plastered to her face, Danny rediscovered the taste of her lips that he remembered from their first kiss.

Sofia pulled away, her eyes boring into his, hands running up and down his chest. "Danny, what happened? Is Santiago okay?"

"He's in jail," Danny said, "but he's fine."

Green looked down and moved dirt with his shoes. The joy fled from Sofia's face. "Jail? But he never wanted to be here."

Danny held her by the shoulders, stroking them gently. "I know, but he was part of the cartel. Agent Green here tells me Santiago will have his chance to share his story. Depending on what all he did while with the cartel, Santiago may have to face a trial."

Sofia looked from him to Agent Green, whom she apparently hadn't seen until now. He offered her a forced grin. "I can actually start by taking your statement. The more you know about your brother being forced to work with the cartel, the better case a defender can make against any charges brought against him."

This was all foreign to Sofia, so she looked to Danny for guidance. He nodded and said, "It's okay. Tell them everything you know. These are the good guys."

"How do you know that?" she asked. "Wasn't the DEA threatening you?"

Danny shot a side eye to Green, who only looked around at the sky. Green really was one of his people. "Agent Green is a friend of a friend and has already done enough today to show his true colors. You can trust him. I promise."

Green smiled at Sofia, who still stared at the FBI agent with a look of hesitation.

"We can even start now," Green said. "If we can find any proof that corroborates your statement, a judge might throw out your brother's case."

Sofia looked at Danny, who nodded again.

"Will I get to see you later?" Sofia asked him.

"I'm not going anywhere today," Danny replied with a grin. "I can't even walk."

He gestured to his ankle, which Sofia hadn't even noticed amid her excitement. "Oh, Danny."

"I'm fine. Go give your statement, and maybe they'll let us get out of here."

"Let's go to my car," Green said, pulling out his notepad again.

Agents were entering and exiting Villa's house with bags of evidence. Villa had yet to be taken out, but Danny knew it was a matter of time before they carried him up the ladder.

"And Mr. Cortez," Agent Green said, handing over a business card. "Let's stay in touch, okay? I'm sure we'll have plenty to discuss."

Danny took the card and tucked it away in his pocket. "Absolutely."

Green and Sofia strolled off together. She looked at Danny over her shoulder, and he nodded to reassure her everything was alright.

Alone on the side of Villa's house, Danny's cell phone buzzed in his pocket. He thought it might be Nadia calling to chop his head off through the phone. But it was a text message from the same blocked number that had been messaging him.

> We knew you could do it. Well done. You will be questioned about our involvement with all this. You are not to speak a word. None of this ever happened. If you leak anything, you'll be sorry.

Danny returned his phone to his pocket and stared out at the desert landscape. Even with Villa now captured and headed back to prison, the question of corruption combined with the text message weighed on Danny.

Someone was still out there. The drama surrounding Los Leones might vanish in the coming months, but more was at play.

As Danny walked away from Villa's house, one thought pressed his mind.

This is far from over.

———

The Story continues in Book 2 of
the Danny Cortez series: Shadow Directive.
Purchase your copy on Amazon!

Not ready to say goodbye? Grab a free Danny Cortez Prequel by
signing up for newsletter at
https://liquidmind.media/danny-cortez-newsletter-signup-1/

THE DANNY CORTEZ SERIES

ALSO BY L.T. RYAN

Find All of L.T. Ryan's Books on Amazon Today!

The Jack Noble Series

The Recruit (free)

The First Deception (Prequel 1)

Noble Beginnings

A Deadly Distance

Ripple Effect (Bear Logan)

Thin Line

Noble Intentions

When Dead in Greece

Noble Retribution

Noble Betrayal

Never Go Home

Beyond Betrayal (Clarissa Abbot)

Noble Judgment

Never Cry Mercy

Deadline

End Game

Noble Ultimatum

Noble Legend

Noble Revenge

Never Look Back

Bear Logan Series

Ripple Effect

Blowback

Take Down

Deep State

Bear & Mandy Logan Series

Close to Home

Under the Surface

The Last Stop

Over the Edge

Between the Lies

Caught in the Web

The Marked Daughter

Beneath the Frozen Sky

Rachel Hatch Series

Drift

Downburst

Fever Burn

Smoke Signal

Firewalk

Whitewater

Aftershock

Whirlwind

Tsunami

Fastrope

Sidewinder

Redaction

Mirage

Faultline

Switchback

Mitch Tanner Series

The Depth of Darkness

Into The Darkness

Deliver Us From Darkness

Cassie Quinn Series

Path of Bones

Whisper of Bones

Symphony of Bones

Etched in Shadow

Concealed in Shadow

Betrayed in Shadow

Born from Ashes

Return to Ashes

Risen from Ashes

Into the Light

Blake Brier Series

Unmasked

Unleashed

Uncharted

Drawpoint

Contrail

Detachment

Clear

Quarry

Dalton Savage Series

Savage Grounds

Scorched Earth

Cold Sky

The Frost Killer

Crimson Moon

Dust Devil

Savage Season

Maddie Castle Series

The Handler

Tracking Justice

Hunting Grounds

Vanished Trails

Smoldering Lies

Field of Bones

Beneath the Grove

Disappearing Act

Silent Witness

Affliction Z Series

Affliction Z: Patient Zero

Affliction Z: Abandoned Hope

Affliction Z: Descended in Blood

Affliction Z : Fractured Part 1

Affliction Z: Fractured Part 2 (Coming Soon)

Alex Hayes Series

Trial By Fire (Prequel)

Fractured Verdict

11th Hour Witness

Buried Testimony

The Bishop's Recusal

The Silent Gavel

Improper Influence

Stella LaRosa Series

Black Rose

Red Ink

Black Gold

White Lies

Silver Bullet

Avril Dahl Series

Cold Reckoning

Cold Legacy

Cold Mercy

Savannah Shadows Series

Echoes of Guilt

The Silence Before

Dead Air

Danny Cortez Series

Dead Man's List

Shadow Directive

Widow Protocol

———

Receive a free copy of The Recruit. Visit:

https://ltryan.com/jack-noble-newsletter-signup-1

ABOUT THE AUTHORS

L.T. RYAN is a *Wall Street Journal* and *USA Today* bestselling author, renowned for crafting pulse-pounding thrillers that keep readers on the edge of their seats. Known for creating gripping, character-driven stories, Ryan is the author of the *Jack Noble* series, the *Rachel Hatch* series, and more. With a knack for blending action, intrigue, and emotional depth, Ryan's books have captivated millions of fans worldwide.

Whether it's the shadowy world of covert operatives or the relentless pursuit of justice, Ryan's stories feature unforgettable characters and high-stakes plots that resonate with fans of Lee Child, Robert Ludlum, and Michael Connelly.

When not writing, Ryan enjoys crafting new ideas with coauthors, running a thriving publishing company, and connecting with readers. Discover the next story that will keep you turning pages late into the night.

Connect with L.T. Ryan
Sign up for his newsletter to hear the latest goings on and receive some free content
➜ https://ltryan.com/jack-noble-newsletter-signup-1

Join the private readers' group
➜ https://www.facebook.com/groups/1727449564174357

Instagram → @ltryanauthor
Visit the website → https://ltryan.com
Send an email → contact@ltryan.com

———

ANDRE GONZALEZ Andre Gonzalez is the international best-selling author of the Wealth of Time Series, and co-owner of M4L Publishing.

After surviving the Aurora Theater Shooting in 2012, Andre was inspired to chase his lifelong dream of pursuing a career as an author. This tragedy gave him a new appreciation for life along with a drive to make the world a better place by publishing books readers all around the world can enjoy.
He has written over twenty time-travel, thriller, and horror books after spending many years reading and studying the works of Stephen King and Dean Koontz. Keeping readers up late and their hearts pumping faster than normal is his ultimate goal. Andre was the recipient of the Rocky Mountain Fiction Writers 2021 Independent Writer of the Year award.

When he's not writing, you can find Andre buried underneath a long to-do list or chasing around his three hyper children. He and his wife are raising their family in their hometown of Denver, CO.

Connect with Andre:

Newsletter - https://andregonzalez.net/join-newsletter/
FB Group - https://www.facebook.com/groups/andregonza lezreaders
FB Page - https://www.facebook.com/AndreGonzalezAuthor
IG - www.instagram.com/monito0408

www.ingramcontent.com/pod-product-compliance
Lightning Source LLC
Chambersburg PA
CBHW060916250626
47159CB00008B/3029